INITIATIVE

TALES OF EROTIC BOLDNESS

EMERALD

MIDNIGHT GLEAM PRESS

Published by Midnight Gleam Press, PO Box 710, Berryville, VA 22611
Edited by Patricia J. Esposito
Cover design by Dawné Dominique of DusktilDawn Designs

ISBN (Print) 978-1-7345991-3-8
ISBN (E-book) 978-1-7345991-5-2

Library of Congress Control Number: 2020904179

This is a work of fiction. "The Beast Within" is a modern retelling of the classic fairy tale "Beauty and the Beast," which is in the public domain. Other than that, names, characters, places, brands, and events were either created from the author's imagination or are used fictitiously with no affiliation with the actual brand or place. With the exception of the comparative reference to Christian Bale in "City Girl," any resemblance to actual persons or events is coincidental and not intended by the author.

"Rules" originally appeared in *Best Erotic Romance 2014*, edited by Kristina Wright (Cleis Press, 2014). "Shift Change" originally appeared in *Best Women's Erotica 2010*, edited by Violet Blue (Cleis Press, 2009). "Lotus" originally appeared in *Best Erotic Romance 2015*, edited by Kristina Wright (Cleis Press, 2015). "Payback" originally appeared in *The Big Book of Orgasms: 69 Sexy Stories*, edited by Rachel Kramer Bussel (Cleis Press, 2013). "The Beast Within (A Modern-Day Fairy Tale)" originally appeared in *Lustfully Ever After: Erotic Fairy Tale Romance*, edited by Kristina Wright (Cleis Press, 2012). "City Girl" originally appeared in *One Night Only: Erotic Encounters*, edited by Violet Blue (Cleis Press, 2012). "Who's on Top?" originally appeared in *G Is for Games*, edited by Alison Tyler (Cleis Press, 2008). "Sunshine" originally appeared in *The One Who Got Away*, edited by Kristina Wright (Cleis Press, 2016). "A Few Hundred Dollars" originally appeared in *Too Fast for Love: Opportunist Encounters* (HarperCollins Mischief, 2012).

CONTENTS

INTRODUCTION

The idea for *Initiative* came as I was mentally reviewing several published stories I knew I'd like to put together into a collection. I noticed they all seemed rather…bold in their premises, and I then noticed that my characters often seemed to embody a kind of straightforwardness in their sexual overtures. (If you know me personally, I'll leave it to you to contemplate whether that is a coincidence.) The word "initiative" occurred to me, and the book took shape from there.

I wrote four new stories to add to the ones I already wanted to include, and as I did, I found a more subtle perception of boldness emerging. Certainly, the openly brazen actions and propositions in stories such as "Shift Change" and "The Beast Within" fit the theme of taking (pretty stark!) initiative, but boldness can take more nuanced forms as well. Within a single individual, historical tendencies and predispositions can make an uncharacteristic choice a distinct act of personal initiative, even if the action itself may appear more mundane to the world at large.

So, somewhat like "vanilla," "kinky," and other words pertaining to the sexual realm, "bold" can be relative. Within these pages, you'll find actions that a majority of the population would probably consider bold, as well as revelations of a more personal nature that, while perhaps less overtly audacious, represent unmistakable initiative for the characters expressing them.

On a personal note, this first-time act of self-publishing undoubtedly reflects a level of initiative historically uncharacteristic of me. In that regard, I join my characters, and I hope—dare I say boldly—you enjoy the result.

Emerald
Virginia 2020

RULES

"What are you doing?"

Joyce looked up to see Pete in the doorway. "Just going through some pictures," she said, looking back down at the disorganized box in front of her. "Many of which I had forgotten I had."

Her husband moved to stand behind where she sat cross-legged on the basement floor. He squinted at the photo in her hand.

"What's that?"

Joyce laughed. "It's when I dyed my hair purple." She held it up for his better viewing.

"You dyed your hair purple?" Pete took the picture from her.

"Yeah. When I was eighteen. I told you that. Didn't I? My parents had a fit."

Pete shook his head, his eyes on the photo.

Strictly forbidden to by her parents, she recalled clearly how she'd grinned the whole time she'd sat in the salon swivel chair the day she turned eighteen, the stylist casually stripping even her light blond hair of its natural color—along with its natural health—to create the foundation for the vibrant hue. The picture had been taken there, right after the hairdresser had finished, by her best friend Chloe. Joyce was smiling into the camera, her shoulder-length hair a shining curtain of violet.

"Hot," Pete said now, handing the picture back to her.

Joyce laughed again. "Really?"

"Yeah." Pete smiled at her. "I like that hair-dyed-funky-color kind of look. I've always had a bit of a thing for the 'rebel goth schoolgirl' character."

"You have?" This was news to her.

"Yeah. Nothing big—just catches my interest a bit. Plus..." he paused, studying the picture over her shoulder again.

"What?"

He shrugged. "Just the attitude. It just looks like dyeing your hair represented something for you. I like that."

Joyce stared down at the picture. He was right. It had.

"Yeah," she said quietly. "I liked it too."

ARRIVING home from work early on Friday, Joyce carried her small shopping bag into the bedroom and knelt to pull the storage boxes out from under the bed. The one she was looking for was toward the middle, requiring the extraction of the more accessible ones in front to reach it.

Flipping the lid off the desired box, she snorted out loud at the few miniskirts and other paraphernalia she'd kept from a time in her life she'd almost forgotten about. They seemed so ridiculously out of place in her life now. She didn't even know why she'd kept them. They were just a few things she hadn't wanted to part with and thought might be handy for Halloween or something sometime.

It hadn't lasted very long, but she had indeed gone

through a bit of a goth phase during her later teenage years. In addition to the purple hair, fishnets, spiderweb tights, patent leather six-inch platform boots, striped wristbands, and approximately a complete pencil of black eyeliner per week had all been part of the picture. She'd had no idea Pete would have any interest in it, so she had never mentioned it to him.

She found the item she was looking for and shook it out. The crunched up vinyl made a snapping sound as it creaked apart. She set the miniskirt on the bed and smoothed it. The silver zipper that ran the entire length of the front had dulled a bit with time.

As she stared at it, she was startled by the visceral memory the garment elicited—like a song, or a smell. Instantaneously she was back at her Floridian studio apartment and the achingly long nights on her feet in a hot, loud, crowded bar. She'd sometimes found it fun at the time, which was hard for her to imagine now.

She reached back to the box and lifted out what had been one of her favorite corsets. The center and back panels were black vinyl, joined by a pattern of horizontal black and white stripes on the sides. Three chunky silver buckles ran up the center.

Shedding her blouse and slacks, Joyce wrapped the skirt around her waist and zipped it up. A little more snug than she remembered, but it still fit. Maneuvering her hands under it, she grasped at her panties and pulled them off. That particular skirt had never gotten along well with undergarments. She wound the corset around her torso and struggled to get the side zipper all the way up. When the corset was finally on, she fluffed her cleavage and pulled out her black-and-white-striped wristbands.

How funny that she and Pete had been married three years and had never known of this commonality between them. Joyce reached into the box and pulled out, one at a time, the black, knee-high, lace-up boots. She looked at them warily. At one time, she had known how to walk in them. Gingerly she lowered her foot into one and zipped it up. She repeated with the other foot and, after adjusting the laces, stood. She was surprised by how natural they felt—appearances aside, their familiarity was unquestionable.

Joyce picked up the bag from Spencer's Gifts. She hadn't entered a Spencer's in years, and being in there had reminded her why. The only patron there that appeared older than twenty-two, she had maneuvered her way through the tight aisles to the back wall and been relieved to see that it was close enough to Halloween for the wigs to be in stock.

She pulled her shiny new costume accessory now from its see-through bag. The style wasn't the same: it was thicker than her hair and had a dense fringe of bangs. But the shade of royal purple was almost identical.

Joyce carried it into the bathroom and brushed it out. It really was a beautiful color. For just a moment she missed wearing it every day, and she smiled at her silliness. Twisting her fair hair up and pinning it as flat as she could against her head, she lifted the wig and carefully maneuvered it over her scalp. Then she began to meticulously outline her eyes in a way she hadn't for more than a decade, smearing jet-black around her eyelids until she somehow gave the impression of a pouty glare regardless of her actual expression. She slathered black mascara over her upper and lower lashes and had to rummage through her makeup drawer quite a bit to locate a tube of blood-red lipstick.

When she was done, she turned to look at herself in the full-length mirror. Her immediate response was to laugh. She was in gleaming black from head to toe, with shining purple polyester framing her face, the bangs of the wig almost reaching her eyelashes as her heavily outlined green eyes blinked back at her. Her lips were the color of ripe cherries.

Wow, I used to look like this all the time on purpose, she thought as she left the bathroom. She made her way down to the basement—carefully, given the six-inch platform heels— and pulled the photo from the top of the box.

She was smiling; she did look happy in the picture. The assertion of Joyce's independence hadn't come with just a hair color change, though Pete was right: it had represented something for her. Her parents never stopped forbidding her to dye her hair, but she had been well aware that their prohibitions would see a hard stop when she turned eighteen. That was the age at which, by law, they didn't get to tell her what to do anymore.

It was one she'd looked forward to for years.

By the end of the summer the picture was taken, Joyce was a couple thousand miles away from the home and family she'd grown up with. She'd taken off and found refuge on the western coast of Florida, eschewing college and making her living as a bartender in the warmth of the state's coastal sun.

Years later, she would go to college because she wanted to, not because she was told she had to.

Joyce looked at the picture, searching for what her husband had seen. Searching for who she'd been back then. Was it different from who she was now?

Of course, life had been different then. She hadn't understood yet what it meant to live on one's own, support oneself financially, do things her parents, however great their ideological differences, had always taken care of for her. Joyce didn't feel, however, that the rebelliousness she'd exhibited and felt so strongly was naive or without worth. Far from it. What she'd done then had been important.

She looked into the beaming gaze staring back at her.

Then she saw it—what her husband had seen when he looked into the same.

It was joy. Pure, simple joy.

Joyce heard Pete come home and tossed the picture back into the box. Lurching toward the stairs, she made her way up them as fast as she could and paused to compose herself at the top. Then she started toward the kitchen where she heard her husband stirring.

PVC creaked as she walked through the house. An involuntary smile lifted her lips; she had forgotten what dressing like this felt like. Her body felt like a pillar, strong and straight, encapsulated snugly in the corset, miniskirt, and boots. The purple wig swished as she strode forward.

Pete did a double take when he saw her. The mail in his hand hung limp as he stared.

It had been a long time since Pete had looked at her like that—since she'd had that kind of effect on him. Joyce was surprised by the rush of arousal that lit up her system. She watched her husband's eyes as they traveled slowly up and down her body, his lips parted in surprise. When he finished and looked back up at her, he appeared at a loss for words. Joyce smiled, and a soft "Wow" finally emerged from his lips.

"Ready to go?" she asked as she stepped forward and linked her arm through his.

"Where?" he managed to get out, showing no inclination to move.

She laughed. "Somewhere we can cause trouble." She winked and pulled him toward the garage door through which he'd just come.

Pete, still staring, didn't answer, and she turned and bent over to pick up her purse. She heard him swallow.

"I don't know what to wear." He said finally, his eyes still on her outfit.

"You wear that," she said, grabbing her coat as she pulled him out the door.

She wound the three-quarter-length trench coat around herself and tied the belt before climbing into the car. As her husband settled into the driver's seat, she noticed the bulge in his pants. He was hard. The revelation took her breath away a little, and the heat she'd felt since he'd caught sight of her surged through her body. She supposed she could have expected it, but she didn't know the last time Pete had gotten hard just looking at her.

"Where do you want to go?"

Where did she want to go? The idea of actually going to a bar, as she would have wanted to back then, brought a slight grimace to her face. She considered. Then her eyes lit up. She bit her lip, sending Pete a sidelong glance. "How about McKinsey's?"

Pete's eyebrows rose. "The hotel?"

Joyce smiled innocently at him. "They have a nice bar there. We could have a drink."

Pete's eyes ran up and down her again in the dark. "Yeah. A drink." He shook himself and started the car. "Works for me."

When they pulled up outside the upscale hotel, a valet opened Joyce's door, and she arranged her coat carefully as she stepped out. Pete walked around to meet her, and it occurred to her that he seemed literally unable to take his eyes off her. Excitement fluttered low in her stomach.

"We're going to skip the drink," Pete murmured as they stepped into the high-ceilinged lobby. Joyce looked at him, secretly thrilled, as he slanted a smile down at her and led them toward the counter that ran along one side of the elegant room. The entrance to the bar was on the other side.

It took a moment for her to realize the sound level had fallen when they'd walked in. Joyce looked around to see a number of people not even hiding the fact that they were staring, and she blushed as she realized she'd been so caught up in her plan that she'd forgotten the kind of reaction her outfit might bring in public. Everyone around her didn't know she was just playing a fun little game with her husband.

Pete showed no sign of disturbance at the stares, and Joyce felt a wave of warmth. If someone had asked her yesterday how she thought her husband might respond to being blatantly stared at and judged by throngs of strangers because of something regarding her, she would have said she wasn't sure. That he was not embarrassed—or at least hid it very well—brought forth a wave of gratitude with a strength that surprised her.

She used to not care either back when she'd dressed like this regularly. Of course, most people then hadn't seemed to —as she recalled, most of the inhabitants of the Florida metropolis where she'd lived hadn't blinked at an eighteen-year-old walking around with bright purple hair and wearing vinyl from head to toe.

This northeastern crowd seemed to expect more from a thirty-something woman on the arm of a man in a business suit. Joyce looked up at Pete; his smile was calm as he met her eyes. She pressed closer to his body as they arrived at the counter and he requested a room from the woman behind it.

Joyce met the receptionist's eyes and at first shrugged off the fact that the woman didn't smile back. As she took Pete's credit card and explained the policies to him in a tight voice, the reason for the cool reception finally dawned on Joyce.

She thinks he's paying me.

The receptionist finished with the transaction and handed Pete their key cards. Joyce was still looking at her, and the woman made eye contact one more time and actually glared at her, clearing her throat pointedly before turning away to reach for the phone. Joyce stood still, shocked by the recognition she'd just undergone but even more shocked by the woman's demeanor. What if he *were* paying her? Would it be that much of a reason to dispose of all customs of politeness and customer service?

Pete put his arm around her, and Joyce clacked with him across the shiny floor to the elevators. The sound level in the lobby had gradually risen, though Joyce didn't doubt that some of the voices they heard were murmuring about them. What a very odd society they lived in. Was it that big a deal if someone wanted to dress differently from the standard nine-to-five cookie-cutter bullshit this city usually reflected? As for the paying-her perception, who gave a shit if she was taking Pete upstairs to fuck him for money? What business was it of theirs?

Joyce felt a slither of the rebellious anger she'd experienced as almost constant in her teenage years. The familiarity was noticeable even as it was tempered—or perhaps complemented—by the fifteen years of life she'd lived between then and now. She was surprised to realize she hadn't felt that energy for a long time. It added something—potency? passion?—to her immediate experience as they reached the elevator bank. It was what made her untie her coat and shrug out of it as they stood waiting for one to arrive. Calmly she folded the garment over one arm, unsure whether the noise level had just lowered a notch again or if it was only her imagination.

An elevator arrived, and they stepped into it. They were alone.

"Jeez, I forgot the kind of reaction wearing this in public might get." Joyce did her best to keep her voice light as the doors closed behind them.

Pete chuckled. "It would be nice to think people had better things to do than worry about what other people are wearing," he agreed, his eyes on the numbers above the door as they beeped with each ascension.

Joyce smiled and moved to hold his hand. He stiffened slightly, and she stopped. "What's the matter?" For a second she feared the public reaction had reached her husband, that he was suddenly looking at her like they had. "Are you embarrassed to be seen with me?" She blurted the words before she could stop herself.

Pete's chuckle turned to a guffaw. With another glance at the numbers, he turned fully toward her, and Joyce felt the heat emanating from his body as he seemed to move closer without taking a step. Joyce fell back a pace at the influx of intensity.

"No, I'm not embarrassed to be seen with you. I'm a little jumpy because you look so fucking hot that I feel like a teenager about to blow a load in my pants just looking at you, and I want to fuck you up against the wall of this elevator right now. Feeling any part of you touch any part of me isn't helping the restraint it's taking not to do that. So what anybody downstairs thought about you or me or the stock market in Asia is just about the furthest thing from my mind right now."

Joyce's jaw dropped. She had never heard Pete talk quite that way before—nor had she heard him use that particular tone. The energy she'd felt in the lobby came flooding back— a mix of arousal, self-possession, power, and freedom. It was a way she was unused to feeling over the last decade, and for a second she was almost light-headed.

The elevator dinged as it halted. Pete grabbed her waist and pulled her close, but just as he appeared about to kiss her, he turned her roughly around and nudged her through the doors, his long strides behind her as they walked down the hall single file. Apparently she wasn't moving quite fast enough for him, because a second later Pete had stopped and scooped her up in his arms, eliciting a gasp of surprise from Joyce, who was aware that anyone they met in the hall now was going to get a clear look of just how few undergarments she had on.

As they reached their door, Pete maneuvered his arm to hand her the key cards he'd been carrying. Joyce pulled one out of the small envelope and slid it into the metal door handle. When the little light turned green, she pulled down on the handle, and Pete shoved the door wide open with one foot.

Somehow it wasn't until that moment that Joyce realized she was breathless, that she had been since the elevator, and that she was all but panting now as her body reminded her that she needed to breathe. At the same time, she became acutely aware of the swelling in her clit and how much she wanted her husband—any part of him—to touch her there. Now.

She was surprised when Pete set her on her feet at the foot of the bed rather than directly on it. Before she could question the move, he launched himself at her and she fell backward onto it anyway, startled—though by this time not surprised—by her husband's urgent carnality. He grabbed her knees and spread her legs, looking at her naked flesh beneath the miniskirt, which had ridden up to her hips without any coaxing. Joyce could feel her wetness as her husband stared at her, and suddenly her urgency matched his.

"Fuck me," she whispered. The purple wig tickled her jawline, but she quickly stopped noticing as Pete struggled out of his pants and crawled back on top of her, his hard cock positioned at the slippery entrance to her pussy. She could feel the tension in his body as he held back, and knowing the effect she was having on him made a rush of arousal spill onto his waiting cock.

Pete sucked in a breath. "I need to be in you now, baby," he panted in her ear. "And I'm going to come fast. Is that okay?"

Joyce was already undulating her hips to desperately try to maneuver him inside her. She would have thought that would be a sufficient answer, but since he seemed to be waiting for one, she hissed out an urgent "Yes" as she spread her legs wider beneath him.

Pete plummeted into her, and she cried out, meeting his thrusts as he fucked her harder, faster, deeper. His hand snaked up and twisted into the purple strands against her cheek, and the way he grunted made her not even mind that he wasn't actually pulling her hair. Though not as satisfying as a true tug on her blond locks, it was obviously having an effect on him, and it was one she wasn't about to argue with.

Joyce's core was a state of pulsing arousal as Pete hammered into her, the feeling of taking her husband's cock more satisfying than it had felt for a long time. His strangled cry indicating that he couldn't hold back anymore almost pushed Joyce over the edge, and she gripped his body with her legs as he came deep inside her. She squeezed him tight, reveling in the power she had to affect him that way.

Breathing heavily, Pete pulled out and rolled over onto his back, reaching for her immediately. He grabbed her waist and pulled her on top of him so she was straddling his torso.

"I'm sorry," he panted.

"Why?"

"Because I didn't let you come first, of course. That's against the rules, isn't it?" His hand slid forward to meet the sheen of sweat and arousal that graced her inner thigh.

"Fuck the rules," she said—and meant it.

She'd looked the way she had in that picture because she had done something she wanted—and had felt, for once, that she truly had the freedom to. The arbitrary orders of someone else didn't apply to her anymore.

That novelty had worn off, it seemed, without her even noticing it. She'd been back in the world of rules now for more than a decade, and she'd forgotten what it felt like to know something she wanted and own the freedom to follow it, to remember she wasn't indebted to somebody's arbitrary rules telling her she couldn't have it. Like wearing vinyl and purple hair into one of the most upscale hotels in the area. Or loving the feeling of her husband's cock in her so much she didn't care that she hadn't had an orgasm yet. Or (she felt on behalf of all who did) getting paid to fuck if that was what she chose to do.

Pete looked in her eyes, and Joyce felt herself beam. For a moment neither of them moved, and Joyce shrieked in surprise when Pete grasped her waist and pulled her forward, the urgency in his forearms not relaxing until she was straddling his face. Before she could catch her breath, she felt the warmth of his tongue connect with her clit.

A low moan broke from her throat, and the tremor that started in her body was electrified by the energy that felt like it was embracing her every cell. Even if she hadn't seen the recognition in her husband's face seconds before, she would have known that her eyes looked exactly as they had in the picture that was the reason they were there. For the first time in a long time, the feeling had enveloped her again, beyond control, pursuit, or even effort.

Joy. Pure, simple joy.

SHIFT CHANGE

I hoisted the shoulder strap on my briefcase as I headed through the mall. When I reached the Apple Store, I walked straight back to the Genius Bar, aka the technical support centers of the Apple world. I had an appointment and was right on time, so I hoped they wouldn't take very long. Being without my computer felt to me like being dropped in the middle of a desert island.

There were no other customers at the Genius Bar, and the "Genius" behind it, his denotation as such announced by his shirt, asked if he could help me as I pulled my MacBook Pro from my briefcase and set it between us. His name tag said "Jake," and I introduced myself and explained that my laptop wasn't getting past the gray loading screen upon startup. He nodded once, businesslike, and plugged in my computer before flipping it open and pushing the power button.

As he did so, I took a closer look at him. Upon first glance I hadn't found him particularly attractive, but as I watched him he began to seem right on the line between classic tech geek and understated sexiness. His expression was serious as he watched the screen, its bright light reflected in the lenses of his glasses as he typed and clicked and probed and whatever else the Apple Geniuses do when someone brings in a problematic computer.

The more I watched him, the more mesmerizing he became. He wasn't the kind of guy I usually found myself attracted to, the kind that turned my head on the street and brought an unsolicited "Fuck me please" forward in my brain. He was the kind that was necessary to watch like this, instigator of a quieter attraction that came out only when all the characteristics that showcased his sexiness—focus, intensity, knowledge—came together for display. Everything about his professional focus and action seemed to flow, but in a very structured manner. Like liquid through a straw.

And suddenly I wanted him to direct that attention at me.

A second Genius appeared behind him, also clad in the telltale shirt. He looked at the screen and said, "Startup trouble?"

"Yeah. I'm checking the hard drive," Jake answered.

The second technician looked at me then and smiled. And my stomach jumped. This *was* the kind of guy I was usually attracted to, the cocky, roughly sexy, hot kind that I wanted to grab me by the hair and shove his cock into me hard. I noted his name tag, which stated "Nick," and introduced myself. The way he looked me up and down elicited heat in me like a volcano, already simmering from my response to Jake. The Apple Store was a hell of a lot more interesting than I had remembered.

Jake continued clicking sporadically and finally looked up at me. "The hard drive is fine, which is good, but it's either a memory problem or the operating system is defunct. It might require a reinstallation, which will mean I'll need to back everything up onto another hard drive first."

I nodded, attempting to look like I had a clue what he was talking about. "Right."

He smiled then. And what a delightful smile he had. It was the first time he had done so, and I smiled back, sheepishly, and shrugged.

"Okay, so I have no idea what you're talking about. But I assume you do."

He chuckled and reached down to pull out a contraption of some sort and a power cord, hooking it all up with the same efficiency with which he had done everything since I started observing him.

Someone sidled up and leaned against the other end of the Genius Bar. "How's it going?" he asked the two behind it. "Busy?"

"Not really," Nick answered. He nodded in my direction. "Stacey here has just brought us her non-starting-up MacBook Pro, which Jake has been working diligently on." His flirtatious sarcasm fit precisely with my impression of him so far—as well as with the image I still had of him holding me down and slamming his cock into me. I smirked and turned to the new arrival.

"Hello, Stacey. I'm Andrew," he said, offering his hand.

I shook it and batted my eyelashes a bit. "You appear to be a Genius too," I said, indicating his shirt. He had an outgoing attractiveness about him, and I was starting to feel like I should come apply for a job in some capacity at the Apple Store.

"Yeah. I'm not on the clock yet though," Andrew said. "I just got here. I don't start for another twenty minutes." He sent me a lazy grin. "So you'll have to get by with these two until then. If they haven't got it figured out by five, I'll take care of it for you."

"It's under control." Jake made his first contribution to the conversation, his eyes not leaving the screen.

"Well, I guess I'll just sit here and talk to you then until it's time for me to go to work," Andrew said with a wink, hoisting himself onto the stool next to me.

I beamed internally, glancing at the two behind the bar working on my laptop, its glowing little apple winking back at me as if to take a sly kind of credit for leading me to this position.

"So is one of you getting ready to leave, then, when Andrew starts?" I asked Jake and Nick.

"Yeah," Nick answered. "I'll be out of here soon."

Jake was mostly ignoring us as he pulled a CD from a drawer beneath him and blew the dust off it before inserting it into my machine. I bit my lip; it was an incredibly sexy gesture coming from him.

"And what about you? Are you almost done or just got here or mid-shift?"

Jake glanced up. "I'm here until close. I'm actually going to go out back for my break when I'm done with this," he added to Andrew.

"Out back?" I couldn't help asking.

"The alley out the back door. It's where Nick and I go for our smoke breaks and Jake goes to get away from people," Andrew said with a laugh. "We seem to be the only ones who ever go out there."

I nodded. I saw the idea immediately as it formed in my head, and I almost laughed at my own predictability.

"It does seem appropriate for you to take a break," I said to Jake, "having been so focused on my computer. Which I appreciate. I imagine you must be ready to toss it out the window about now."

Jake smiled as he moved his fingers over the track pad, his eyes on the screen. "It's my job."

"Your place out back sounds intriguing," I continued. "I guess at least one of you has to be here all the time, though, which dashes my idea of a little impromptu gangbang there."

Nick and Jake looked up at me in unison. It was the most I had seen Jake's attention pulled from my computer since I had come in. I smiled, and Nick guffawed. All three relaxed as they interpreted my comment as a joke.

My lighthearted smile had been orchestrated for that result—I was just testing the environment. It seemed to me that while they thought I had been joking, it had caught their interest. I determined there was enough of it there for me to proceed. I hoped so, anyway.

I laughed with them. "So you're about to go on break, Jake, Nick's about to get off work, and you haven't started yet," I said, turning to Andrew.

Andrew looked at me. I could tell he was wondering what I was getting at, and I decided to eliminate all suspense. I met his eyes.

"So if I went out back and stood against the wall where I imagine you stand outside and smoke your cigarettes, you could all come out one at a time and fuck me."

Jake and Nick, who had both returned to my computer, missed this comment as they talked among themselves, my supposed comical remark forgotten for the time being. Only Andrew, who was still focused on me, looked at me in disbelief.

I gave him a sidelong glance. "Since you appear to be the only one paying attention at this point, and since you're not on the clock yet, you could go first," I suggested. "Don't worry, I have condoms in my purse."

Andrew's expression didn't change, and I felt a twinge of disappointment as I thought he might turn the offer down. He may have been thinking about his job, or he might have been uncomfortable with the three of them sharing such information.

"You really want us to do that?" he finally asked.

"Do you think I'd sit here and ask if I didn't?" I said with a little laugh. "It even works out well numerically—there are three of you, and there are three places I can think of in which I'd love to be penetrated."

Nick and Jake happened to be at a lull in their own conversation at that moment, and they both looked up with a start, their stares lingering this time.

"You've missed part of the conversation," I said to them. "I was just about to ask Andrew to show me where to meet you all out back, but I think I can figure it out. Since one of you needs to be here all the time, you'd have to come do me one at a time. I've already invited Andrew to go first. The three of you can decide among yourselves which one of you gets to fuck my mouth, which one gets my pussy, and which one gets my ass. I, incidentally, will run over to the drugstore across the street and pick up lube." I smiled at my practicality even under the circumstances. I turned to Andrew. "So I'll meet you out back in about five minutes. And if you decide you're not interested," I added to the group at large, "no hard feelings."

I slipped away from the Genius Bar and out into the mall. After completing the requisite trip to the drugstore, I reentered the mall and passed by the Apple Store, stealing a glance inside at the back. Jake and Nick were side by side behind the bar, apparently still working on my computer. Andrew was missing.

I walked to the mall exit closest to the store, which happened to not be a public one. I pushed through one of the double metal doors and let it slam behind me. The gray expanse of concrete in front of me was deserted. I turned to the left and rounded the corner a few yards away. I saw Andrew immediately, standing against the wall beside a single gray door and smoking a cigarette. He turned and saw me.

He appeared nervous, but all I felt at that point was hot. The back of the gray building was vacant except for the two of us, just as they had said.

I walked up to him, and Andrew turned to me, never breaking eye contact as he dropped his cigarette and crushed it out with his boot. I didn't break stride until I was touching him, my lips devouring his, the smell of cigarette smoke fresh in the cold fall air. His response held no hesitation, and his arms wrapped around me, his hands roaming from my ass up to my neck and through my hair. I normally hated cigarette smoke, but I loved the way he was touching me so much that at that moment it barely fazed me.

"So where are you going to fuck me?" I whispered.

Andrew sucked in his breath, and I reached down and felt the hard cock beneath his zipper.

"Your pussy," he whispered back.

I smiled. Somehow this choice didn't surprise me. Wishing I had worn a skirt, I quickly unfastened my jeans and pushed them down, stepping out of them and leaving my boots on. I shimmied out of my panties as well while he watched me.

"You're going to have to undo your pants, too," I said with a smile as Andrew stood mesmerized. He jumped a little, then gave me a self-conscious grin as he reached for his zipper.

His cock sprang out, and I rolled the condom I had extracted from my purse down onto it. Then I backed up at the same time he moved toward me, and our bodies came together just as my back hit the concrete wall. Raising one leg, I pressed my knee into his hip, and he grabbed the back of my thigh and entered me with a thrust.

My head went back against the rough stone behind me,

and I bit my lip to keep from screaming. I could feel the wetness on my thighs as he pumped into me, breathing heavily and not speaking. I met his eyes, still suppressing the moans wanting to break from my throat, as he pushed his cock into me over and over, his pace increasing with his breath as he got closer to orgasm. Finally I could take it no more and pushed my face into his shoulder, letting my scream be muffled by his flesh. His breathing got harsh as he came in me, pumping with abandon as his body jerked and his hand gripped the flesh of my shoulder.

He pulled out and gazed at me, appearing at a loss for words.

"Thank you," I said, giving him a wink.

He smiled, and I smiled back. He moved forward to kiss me quickly, then backed away, lifting his hand in a small wave as he disappeared through the gray metal door. By the time it closed heavily behind him, I was pressing my clit, making myself come within seconds of his exit. I was still breathing heavily when the door scraped open again and Jake stepped out, smiling faintly as he met my eyes.

"You look like you're ready to go," he said as he stood before me. He appeared just the way he had while working on my computer: straightforward, focused, businesslike. Even under the present circumstances the polish was still there.

It made me just as hot as I had thought it would.

I chuckled breathlessly and found that I was too aroused and out of breath to even formulate words. Jake's focused expression took on a lustful tenor as he reached down and unbuckled his belt. His eyes stayed on me as he undid his pants and pulled his cock out. Without instruction, I knew what part of me he had chosen to penetrate.

I smiled and dropped to my knees, taking his cock in my mouth and looking up at him as he drew in a quick breath.

Knowing I only had a few minutes, I sucked hard and fast, taking his cock all the way in, growing wetter with every pump. Momentarily I drew back, saliva joining my lips and his cock as I looked up at him.

"I like this a little rough," I whispered. "So if you have no objections, I would be delighted if you would grab my hair and push my head onto your cock when you come."

Jake's cool demeanor almost slipped as his mouth opened slightly and his eyes half closed. I resumed sucking his dick, and he snaked a hand around to the back of my neck. He grunted quietly as he acquiesced, gripping my hair with both hands and shoving my head forward rhythmically as his hot come started to spurt into my mouth. I looked up at him and gripped the base of his cock, stroking as I let his come run down my chin and across my lips.

When he was done, I smiled. He did too, coolly, and backed up as he tucked his cock back into his pants.

"Thanks," he said, reaching down to help me to my feet. He met my eyes. "You suck one hell of a cock." For the first time, his voice was rough, and I thought I might come at the sound. With a nod, he turned toward the door. "See you inside."

I smiled, still breathless with arousal. Which was good, since I was about to get my ass fucked. I pulled a tissue out of my purse to clean the come off my face, then reached for the bag from the drugstore and pulled out the bottle of lube.

Nick emerged from the door moments later.

"Hi," he said. "Your laptop's almost ready."

Oh, yes, my laptop. I nearly laughed as I realized I had almost forgotten about it—the reason I was here.

Nick stepped toward me. Rather than the understated confidence and professionalism of Jake or the charming, slightly nervous appreciation of Andrew, Nick exuded more of the kind of cockiness that usually made me salivate.

The present circumstances were no exception.

"So my understanding is that I get to fuck your ass," he said.

"That's right." I held up the bottle of lube.

"Well, I certainly appreciate that," Nick said as he took it. "I haven't fucked anyone's ass for a long time. I sure didn't think I'd get the chance when I came to work today."

"Well, what a lovely coincidence." During this exchange, I had pulled another condom from my purse and torn it open, and he had already freed his cock from his jeans. I looked down and slid the condom on, then glanced back up at him before turning around and bending over, planting my palms against the rough gray surface of the wall.

Nick made an approving noise as I felt him move closer to me. I heard the bottle of lube flip open, and then I felt Nick's cock nudging between my ass cheeks, stopping before he penetrated me.

"I don't know how used to this you are, so I'll take my cues from you," he said. His voice was tight with arousal. I nodded and backed up slowly, pushing myself around the head of his cock and inching my way back against him until he was all the way inside my ass. I let out a breath, arching my back as the physical sensation and pure carnality of what we were doing shot straight to the pit of my stomach.

I could tell by Nick's breathing that he was experiencing something similar. I moved slowly back toward the wall, then back up against him, sliding his cock in and out of my ass slowly as I set the pace. When I was ready, I turned my head.

"Okay," I whispered. "You can go ahead now."

Nick pushed into me firmly, though keeping the pace not much faster than I had set it. He moaned quietly, reaching down once to slap my ass as he took it from behind. I gasped with pleasure and met his strokes, pushing back against him until I heard him grunt through clenched teeth and knew he was coming. He gripped my hips, and I felt the wetness again between my thighs as he climaxed into me.

Nick surprised me then by reaching around in front of me with his right hand and finding my clit, stroking me there delicately as he pulled out of my ass and held me in place by my hip. I moaned, unable to keep quiet as he made me come, smacking my ass once again as he pressed his fingers firmly against my clit.

I turned with a surprised smile. "Thank you."

He grinned. "Oh, thank *you*." He winked at me as he refastened his pants, then watched as I gathered my jeans and panties.

"You can go ahead," I told him. "I'll be right in."

I pulled my clothes on quickly and walked back around the corner, entering through the door from which I had exited. I stopped at the restroom to do some cleanup, then headed back through the mall to the Apple Store. I walked in and went straight back to the Genius Bar, where Jake and Andrew now stood huddled over my laptop. Nick was off to the side, presumably preparing to depart.

Andrew saw me first and smiled shyly. Jake looked up then as well, his penetrating gaze resting on mine.

"How's it going?" I asked casually, nodding at the laptop in front of them.

"We're running a test on it now, and that should take care of it. Should be done in just a second," Jake said.

"Don't let that stop you from coming back to see us anytime there's anything we can do for you, though," Nick said from my left with a grin.

My chuckle was a little breathless. I wasn't sure how I would be handling the temptation to do exactly that as I accepted my laptop from Jake and slipped it back into my briefcase. I thanked the three of them and felt them watching me as I turned and wound among the computer-laden counters and bustling customers toward the exit.

As I approached it, I smiled recalling the direness I had felt about being without my computer when I first entered the store. Forty-five minutes of tension relief later, I found myself wondering what might next go wrong with the laptop I carried at my side. Amazing what those Geniuses could do.

LOTUS

It was time for a brand-new one. Though Charlotte loved all stages of her favorite hobby, breaking out an unopened box and turning it upside down over the table held an undeniable special rush. As the one thousand carved cardboard pieces heaped onto the wood surface, she stood the box lid up to her left and began to spread them out and flip them so they were all shiny side up.

Charlotte's gaze surveyed the jumble of what looked like chaos in front of her, a part of her psyche already resting with the confidence of seeing the order. It hadn't manifested yet, but that part of her knew it was there. She had developed a sense of perception around the details in a puzzle's picture that afforded her a solid assurance that however challenging a puzzle seemed—and they were all challenging in their own way—the pieces of any one could always be put together. It was one of the things she loved most about puzzles: they could, by their nature, invariably be mastered.

As she finished flipping the pieces, Charlotte scoured the table, seeking the straight edges among the myriad curves and angles. In the years she'd been doing them, puzzles had developed into almost a companion in her life, a steadfast focus that was always renewable. She started and finished puzzles the way some people started and finished reading books. She'd even been known to time things according to them. It had been almost exactly a year ago, for instance, that she'd made the internal agreement that she would move out of Ralph's condo when she finished the thousand-piece farm scene. Ralph had worked on it alongside her sometimes, Charlotte's stomach continually clenching with the secret knowledge of what their progress meant as they pieced together the faded red barn with horses grazing in the foreground.

At the time, the impending action had felt excruciating; now it was like a passing breeze, a memory that made her glance up for just a second before focusing again on the fresh underwater scene in front of her.

Charlotte's cell phone rang as she caught sight of the first corner. Not recognizing the number, she debated whether or not to answer as she spotted a second corner. Sliding the piece toward her with one finger, she picked up and answered the phone with her other hand.

"Hello?"

"Hi, this is Gavin Shannon, calling in response to your email inquiry on my website." The voice was smooth and professional, and Charlotte instantly recognized the name of the photographer whose site she had encountered the day before.

"Oh, yes, hi," she said. "Thanks for calling back."

"Of course. I am available to do a shoot at the botanical gardens you mentioned, and I'd be happy to set up a time."

"Oh, great." Charlotte pulled the third corner toward her and moved a few edge pieces to their appropriate side before realizing she wasn't paying attention to the voice that was now talking about rates and scheduling.

"Tomorrow?" she asked, catching the word as she sat back and did her best to shift her attention. "Yes, I could do that. I have no idea how long this might take or anything like that. There's just a particular thing I'd like a photo of, and I don't take pictures well enough to do it justice."

Gavin laughed warmly. "Something tells me you may underrate yourself," he said, his voice light, "but again, I'm more than happy to help you out."

For some reason Charlotte almost felt herself blush. It was a charming compliment, and despite his knowing nothing about her, he had somehow managed to make it sound sincere.

She said goodbye and set the phone beside her on the table. Though Charlotte loved the idea of personalized puzzles, she had only had two made from her own photographs. One was a close-up of a pale pink peony bush, in full majestic bloom outside her grandparents' house several years ago. The framed puzzle had hung in their dining room until they'd both passed away. Then it had reverted back to her possession, where it hung now above the fireplace.

The other was of her beloved cocker spaniel mix, Lucky, who'd died two years before at the age of sixteen. The framed portrait of him she'd painstakingly put together—it had, somehow, worked like a slow channeler of her grief, though she hadn't been able to even touch it until more than a month after his death—was on the wall above her bed. She still remembered the moment she'd captured the image. Lucky had rolled onto his back, his madly wagging tail blurry as it wiggled like a furry snake along the ground. To this day, Charlotte's heart lurched a tiny bit every time she caught sight of the framed puzzle that was easily the most meaningful she had ever put together.

Still, Charlotte knew she was no photographer. It didn't

seem that hard—just aim the camera at what she wanted a photo of and push the button—but her lack of success in deriving the desired outcome from doing just that indicated how much more there was to photography than she understood. It was a skill she admired greatly.

The lotus puzzle was something she wanted to do for Connie. Perhaps it would lift her spirits. If not, Charlotte hoped that at the very least it would help her feel supported. Connie hadn't been very far along when the miscarriage had happened, and Charlotte knew her best friend hadn't found it as heart-wrenching as she might have. But she knew too that it had been a very wanted pregnancy, and Connie's pain had been evident enough when Charlotte had gone to see her after she'd gotten the call last week.

The pond at the local botanical gardens was one of Connie's favorite things, and Charlotte had seen the lone pink lotus flower a couple days before during a solitary visit. She'd snapped her own picture with her cell phone camera, but it hadn't done justice to the splendor of the blossom as it graced its lily pad with a kind of transcendence. Charlotte didn't even own a "real" camera and realized that for what she wanted to do, it would be best to hire a professional.

Despite her eagerness only moments before, Charlotte felt a bit restless now as she looked down at the pieces in front of her. Pushing aside the notion that the phone conversation she'd just had was responsible for the inexplicable butterflies, Charlotte pushed back from the table and headed for the stairs, deciding to indulge in her second-favorite pastime before getting back to the new puzzle. She grabbed a towel, passed through the bedroom, and reached for the tap of her beloved oversized bathtub.

WHEN SHE EMERGED from her car the following day, Charlotte caught sight of a figure crossing the parking lot from the other side. Squinting, she made out a black camera bag slung over the man's shoulder and stopped to wait on the sidewalk.

As he drew closer, Charlotte's stomach dropped a little. Even with a winter coat on, Gavin's figure evidenced a solid build, muscular but graceful. His dark hair framed classic features arranged in a friendly, open expression as he approached. He smiled when he caught her eye.

"Hi. You must be Charlotte? I'm Gavin."

He extended his hand, and Charlotte took it automatically, trying to find her tongue.

"Of course. It's a pleasure to meet you," she finally managed, trying to calm the fluttering in her stomach as they headed toward the door. Gavin held it for her, and Charlotte ducked out of the bitter wind into the slight shock of the hot, humid atmosphere of the greenhouse.

"This heat feels great for about three seconds, then it gets a little overwhelming to the other extreme," Charlotte said with a breathless laugh as they hung their coats on the rack inside the door.

Gavin smiled. "I'm sure I can handle it. I'm from San Antonio originally."

"Really? You don't have much of an accent."

He chuckled. "I went to college in Minneapolis, and it eventually went away for the most part. You may still catch me calling you 'ma'am' on occasion, though."

Charlotte smiled and led the way to the pond, biting her lip as she caught a whiff of his aftershave. "Did you go to school for photography?"

"Yep. I minored in business, though, in case I needed something to fall back on." He laughed as they neared the water. "Is this the pond?"

"Yes. There's a lotus blooming in the middle of it, and I want a picture of it to make into a puzzle."

"Really? What a cool idea. Sounds like extra work, though…why don't you just have it blown up and frame it?"

"I love doing puzzles," Charlotte answered, feeling a bit self-conscious. It sounded a little silly put like that. "This one is for a friend, actually. She loves this place. I think it'll just give it more of a…personal touch. She and her husband went through a challenge recently, and I want to do this to support her."

Gavin glanced at her. "That's awesome," he said as she stopped in front of the water. "Beautiful," he murmured, peering over the short stone wall separating it from the path as his hands went to his camera.

"Yes," she agreed. "I'm not sure if I want something relatively close-up with just a few of the lily pads around it, or one that's further back so she can identify the pond.…"

"I'll take some of both," Gavin said, already starting to aim and click a few feet away from her. Charlotte sensed a shift in him as he began to work. His attention went fully to the contraption in his hands, the eye nearest her squeezed shut as he varied the camera's angle and snapped several pictures in a row.

"It's so amazing to see things like this blooming in here when it's literally freezing outside," Charlotte said after a while.

Gavin was walking back and forth along the path in almost a kind of dance, repositioning his tripod and snapping pictures from different angles. "Yeah. Some lotus species can survive colder temperatures, though not as cold as it is here. They can keep themselves in bloom down to about fifty degrees, though."

"Really?"

"Yeah. They're able to regulate their temperature to some

degree—no pun intended. They can heat their own blossoms when it's colder out to attract the pollinators they need to reproduce."

Charlotte stared at him. "I had no idea any plant could do such a thing."

Gavin shrugged as he adjusted the tripod, pointing the camera toward the pond and clicking away. "I think we underestimate a lot about plants. How they fit in to the whole ecosystem thing. My sister's a master gardener at one of the park systems in Maryland. I probably know more about plants than the average person from hearing her talk about them." He pushed the shutter one last time and straightened to face her. "Any other angles you want me to hit?"

The question made her cheeks tinge pink for some reason, and she shook her head.

"So won't it take you a while to put the puzzle together?" Gavin asked as they walked back to the exit.

Charlotte shrugged. "Depends on what you mean by 'a while.'"

Gavin snorted. "I think it took me about a year to finish the last jigsaw puzzle I did. That was probably sometime when I was a teenager, maybe even younger." He gave her a crooked smile that seemed a bit self-deprecating. She remembered her own self-consciousness and felt strangely touched that he appeared to care how she might see that.

"I think it's like a lot of things in that the more you do it, the better—or in this case, faster—you get at it."

She was finding Gavin easier to talk to than anyone she'd met in a while. When they reached the coatrack, he grabbed her coat and helped her into it. Charlotte caught her breath as his hand brushed hers. She slipped her arms quickly into the sleeves.

"Thank you. That's very southern-gentlemanly of you," she teased.

She thought she saw Gavin blush himself then, but he turned and reached for his own coat before she could tell for sure. They took a moment to bundle up, and Gavin held the door open as Charlotte stepped out into the biting cold and the glass swung shut behind them.

Two days later Charlotte left work early, wanting to get home before the foot of snow predicted for the evening started to fall. Visual evidence of the previous night's ice storm still covered the non-road surfaces as she entered her neighborhood. Crystalline shards of fallen ice littered the ground beneath larger trees, and the bushes lining the road looked as though they had aged overnight, sprouting identical heads of icy white hair.

She wasted no time drawing a hot bath when she arrived home. Sighing contentedly, Charlotte sank into the liquid heat and looked up at the large windows that framed the corner tub. The temperature difference inside and out was drastic enough that the glass had steamed up, but she could still make out the first of the snow starting to fall beyond it. As she watched the flakes grow thicker, Charlotte pictured the lotus bloom, delicate and protected from the scathing winter temperatures inside its giant glass dome. An image of the photographer who had accompanied her to see it followed, and she shivered a little despite the warmth surrounding her.

The phone on the tile ledge beside her rang, and she turned her head to check the number. The buzz in her stomach grew stronger.

Pushing herself up, she quickly towel-dried her hands and leaned over the edge of the tub to answer. "Hello?"

"Hi, it's Gavin. I hope you're staying warm in this imminent blizzard."

Charlotte's breath caught. "I am warm indeed," she said, noting that his tone of voice would almost certainly have done the trick even if she hadn't been submerged in heated water.

Gavin chuckled. "Well, I'm calling because I have your proofs here and wanted to see if you wanted to come by the studio on your way home to take a look at them."

Charlotte felt a stab of disappointment as she explained that she was already home for the day due to the forecast. "I'm terrible at driving in snow," she said with a self-conscious laugh.

"I understand." Gavin paused. "I'd be happy to come to you if you'd like. I can close up here any time and bring them by your place."

The butterflies in Charlotte's belly jumped in unison.

"Okay," she said, managing to keep her cool. "Of course, that means you'll have to drive more in the snow yourself—and you might even get stuck here." She bit her lip, realizing she could think of worse things than having to host Gavin for the night.

"True," he said casually. "But my truck is four-wheel-drive, and I got pretty used to driving in the snow when I lived in Minnesota. If you're worried about it, though, we can wait a day or two." Gavin sounded like he was smiling.

"No, that's okay," Charlotte said, smiling too. She gave him her address and hung up the phone, then carefully set it back on the ledge before climbing out of the tub.

Downstairs, she ran her eyes around the living room. Her "puzzle table," as she called it, was the centerpiece of one half of the sunken room, with the other half devoted to a couch and love seat facing each other perpendicular to the brick fireplace. She had forgone a coffee table in favor of end tables flanking each piece, preferring the open space in front of the fireplace that was covered with her grandparents' antique rug. She flipped a switch on the wall, and a small burst of flames materialized behind the fireplace glass.

As a potential preparation occurred to her, Charlotte bit her lip, wondering if she was being overambitious. Finally she rolled her eyes and dashed from the room, returning with two condoms that she slipped into the small drawer in the end table closest to her. Her cheeks burned as she told herself she was probably hugely misreading Gavin's intentions in coming there. Still, might as well be on the safe side.

The doorbell rang, and Gavin smiled at her as he stepped inside. His eyes swept over the room as he removed his boots, and he smiled wider when he saw the puzzle table.

"Do you always have one in progress?" he asked, walking over to look at the partially finished underwater scene.

"Usually," she answered. "May I take your coat?"

Gavin shrugged out of it, revealing a smart black button-down shirt over jeans, which he filled out ridiculously well. Charlotte turned and carried his coat to the closet, willing the blush she could feel in her cheeks to subside.

"I wouldn't even know where to start," Gavin murmured as she returned to the table, his eyes running over the pieces. "How do you even begin to put this thing together?"

"Well, first you find the four corners. Then you look for the edges and work on the border until it's done—or I do, at least. I then sort the pieces according to approximately where they go, which I haven't really gotten to yet on this one.

"The thing is, there's a way to look at every piece and then study the box picture and match at least one particular detail—thus figuring out where the piece goes. Even if no pieces are yet together in the vicinity, I can usually look at one and find a detail on it that matches the picture and place it at least in the area where it will eventually go.

"Take this piece," she continued, picking up one that was a combination of turquoise and a textured-looking red.

She studied the picture for several moments. Gavin didn't say anything, but she sensed him watching closely. Eventually she found it. "So it goes right about here," she said, placing the piece in an empty spot inside the puzzle's border. Picking up the box lid, she pointed at the picture. "I can't fit it in yet because the pieces around it aren't in place, but it's this edge of the red starfish with water behind it. See the way the angle in the piece matches the one in the picture right there, and the little bumps on the starfish are arranged the same way?"

"That's quite an eye for detail."

Charlotte set the lid down. "Well, you must have that kind of perception, too, right, as a photographer?"

Gavin looked thoughtful. "I'm not sure it's the same. I think I see whole pictures rather than details. I don't usually see something and identify all the little things about it that make it up. I just look at something and know I like what I see." Charlotte felt a tingle rush through her as his eyes flicked almost imperceptibly up and down her. "And usually that's when I start taking pictures."

"I guess that makes sense," Charlotte said. "After all, I can put a puzzle together but don't know the first thing about taking a decent picture." She laughed and glanced at the peony puzzle hanging above the fireplace.

Gavin followed her gaze.

"I took that one," she said a bit nervously before he could ask. "That's one of only two puzzles I've had made out of photos of my own."

"Now, see, that's a beautiful shot," Gavin drawled, a touch

of southern accent tinging his words as he stepped closer to the frame. He pushed his hands into his pockets as he gazed up at it, and Charlotte bit her lip as she studied his form from behind.

"Would you like to sit down?" She gestured at the furniture and fidgeted internally, not sure whether to initiate sitting on the love seat or stay with the safety of the couch. She decided to let him choose and hung back.

Gavin hesitated, then headed for the couch. He sat somewhat near the middle of it, and Charlotte sat on one side, not quite up against the arm but not on top of him, either.

"I hope you find something that works in these," he said as he pulled a batch of prints out of his bag.

"I'm sure I will." Without meaning to, Charlotte drifted closer to him as she looked at the first print over his shoulder.

Her lips parted as she took in the electrifying hues of one of the most pristine images she'd ever seen. Layers of emerald lily pads reached to each edge of the photo and glistened like they were lacquered, offering a backdrop for the graceful cluster of petals that rose like a velvet fire in nuanced shades of pink she hadn't begun to notice when she'd looked at it in person. Every surface seemed to rise off the page like it was close enough to be touched; the water droplets on the leaves looked as though they might burst any second.

"Oh," she breathed, taking the photo from him. After a few moments, she accepted the next print he handed her. This one, too, was stunning, depicting the lotus bloom from the other side, with a bit of the pond visible in one corner and a more prominent view of the fringed yellow seedpod.

Gavin handed her a third one. It was one of the distance shots, the frame encompassing the surrounding water and foliage that bordered the pond. The lotus itself was just off-center, complemented by a background of tall yellow flowers that laced the far end of the pond, draping green branches of the tree that hovered over the right side of the water, and a section of the jagged rock wall that extended around the pond to the left. The lotus sat alone among its lily pads, like a beacon in a sea of shiny green splendor.

Charlotte looked at the picture for a long time, knowing the location would be instantly recognizable to Connie. "These are amazing," she said finally, tearing her eyes from the photo to look up at him.

She caught a look in his eyes she wasn't sure she was supposed to see. Gavin was watching her deeply, intensely—hungrily. Though she worried she'd caught him doing something he hadn't wanted her to, he didn't look away, but rather cleared his throat and smiled as he sat back against the cushions.

"I'm so glad you think so. It was beautiful subject matter, of course. You have good taste."

His eyes, Charlotte thought, still looked hungry. Finding herself a tiny bit breathless, she glanced away and said, "Can I get you something to drink?"

"Sure." Gavin got up and followed her to the kitchen as she started listing what she had in the fridge. As she reached it, her gaze flicked to the window, and she paused.

"Snow's really coming down," she said, a note of concern in her voice as she watched the flurry of white on the other side of the glass. "I hope you'll be able to get out okay. I'll feel really bad if you get stuck here." She turned back to him, realizing the words weren't altogether true.

Gavin laughed, glancing behind her out the window. "I can think of worse things," he said lightly.

Charlotte felt as though her breath had been pulled out from underneath her as he met her eyes again, the combination of hunger and restraint more subtle now but still there. Flustered, she gestured behind her to the refrigerator.

"So, what would you like?"

Gavin was standing a few feet away, but he moved slowly toward her as she watched him. Giving her plenty of time to move had she wanted to, he finally said in a low voice, "You."

The moment froze. Then he was kissing her, pressing her back against the counter as his body pushed into hers. Charlotte's breath vanished, and heat shot straight from her belly to her cunt as Gavin reached his arms around her and pulled her somehow closer. A tiny moan spilled from her throat, and she found herself willing their clothes to simply disappear.

Gavin stepped back just far enough to lift her off her feet, and seconds later he was lowering her back onto the couch in the living room. Charlotte arched her back as he climbed on top of her, his movements somehow urgent and measured at the same time.

She ground herself against him, and Gavin groaned as he rose to his knees, almost ripping the buttons on his shirt in his haste to get them undone. Charlotte sat up and pulled off her sweater, falling back to the cushions as she dropped it on the rug beside them.

Gavin breathed heavily as his eyes ran over her body. The carnal lust in them made Charlotte greedy for his touch, and she grabbed his hands, pressing one to her breast and pulling the other to her mouth. She ran her tongue over his fingertips, and Gavin's breath hissed when she pulled one into her mouth, sucking hungrily as he reached beneath her and unsnapped her bra. Pulling it off roughly, he leaned down and latched his teeth over a nipple, making her cry out.

Charlotte reached down and ran a strong hand over Gavin's denim-covered erection, and he pulled back to wrench his pants open. When he jumped up to pull them off,

Charlotte stared at the diamond-hard cock in front of her, unable to stop herself from rising to her knees and taking it into her mouth. She sucked it like she had his finger, and Gavin moaned, clenching his fists at his sides. In a moment she felt his hand against her head, not pushing but rather pulling her hair gently away from him.

"You'll make me come," he whispered, panting as he looked down at her. "And I want to be inside you for that."

Charlotte rose up so she was at eye level with him, on her knees on the couch as he stood beside it. She held his gaze for a beat, then stretched over to the small drawer in the end table. Returning to her previous position, she pressed the small square into Gavin's hand and said quietly, "Get there, then."

Gavin pushed her back down on the couch, tearing open the wrapper and sliding the condom on in one frantic motion as he knelt between her legs and pulled her into position by her thighs. Charlotte felt the moisture between them as she lifted her hips, willing him to plunge inside her.

He complied. She cried out as he entered her, and though she still sensed the restraint in his hard muscles as she gripped his arms, it seemed he soon couldn't help himself and started fucking her with abandon as she screamed with similar unrestraint. Words came from her mouth that surprised her, encouraging him to pound her wet cunt and make her take his hard cock and fuck her harder, faster, deeper. She would have been blushing if she hadn't been so consumed by things more important than decorum.

Suddenly reining himself in, Gavin pulled back and knelt above her. She could feel his hardness pulsing inside her as he pressed her clit with his thumb. She came almost instantly with an unabashed scream, and Gavin rocked his hips forward and pumped into her for mere seconds before he followed suit, groaning her name as he emptied himself inside her.

When he pulled out, Gavin met her eyes and gently leaned down to kiss her, adjusting himself on the couch so their bodies fit side by side. She felt his breath against her hair as the air cooled around them. After a moment, Charlotte's soft voice broke the silence.

"I think you'd better stay here tonight no matter what the weather does."

She felt him smile, the words warm against her skin as he murmured into her shoulder, "I think you're right."

CHARLOTTE CARRIED the silver 8x10-inch frame into the bathroom and set it on the ledge along the tub. Lifting the hammer, she pounded the picture hanger into the wall across from the windows, then retrieved and carefully hung the brilliant close-up of the shimmering lotus blossom.

She had already placed an order for the exquisite distance shot to be made into the puzzle for Connie. This photo, however, would remain in one piece, its dazzling hues and piercing details a perpetual witness to her cherished time in the tub—starting with tonight's. Charlotte felt the heat of anticipation as she leaned down and turned on the tap, testing the temperature for a few seconds before twisting the stopper into place. As she straightened, the doorbell rang. Charlotte dried her hands and ran downstairs to let Gavin in.

PAYBACK

I drove by slowly, running my eyes over the nine-story hotel less than six months old. Its staunch exterior brimmed with newness, solidity, progress. My gaze dropped to the ground floor, where the foundation of the building covered the worn abandoned parking lot where I'd sucked him off so many times those years ago, on my knees on the pavement as he'd panted in the driver's seat.

Before I knew better, I thought.

It had been six years. Six years in which a lot could—and had—happened.

I'd been eighteen then, in almost no possession of any understanding of what I wanted sexually, much less that I had the right to ask for it. It wasn't that I hadn't enjoyed our one-sided exploration—still today, giving head was one of my favorite things.

No, what struck me as I pulled my gaze back to the road was that it hadn't occurred to me to even *want* any more. Wistfulness tinged with sadness flitted over me as I ached for that girl I was, who didn't know enough to demand her part in the rendezvous pattern that summer. Who instead jumped out of her car night after summer night and ran giggling over to his, dutifully sucking him off as he moaned blissfully, his heavy hands tangled in her hair.

Phillip was older and had been more experienced than I at the time. Whether my own pleasure hadn't occurred to him or he exploited my lack of knowing, I didn't know. It had occurred to me since then that it was probably the latter. Looking back, it admittedly fit with the rest of the impression I had of him.

I KNEW his voice even before I turned.

"Hello, Phillip."

I'd known I would see him while I was here—it was too small a place to avoid it. Granted, the parking lot of the ice cream shop directly across the street from a certain new hotel wasn't the most inconspicuous place I could have hidden, had I wanted to.

"I heard you were in town. Glad I ran into you." Phillip's eyes flicked to the building at which I had just been staring, and I could hardly imagine he wasn't recalling the same things I had when I'd driven by the night before.

He was still hot, though the swaggering "bad boy" demeanor didn't do as much for me now as it had back then. His blond hair fell almost to his eyes, and the athletic frame he'd sported six years ago was still intact.

His eyes ran up and down me as his grin grew a little wider. He walked in front of me and leaned against the wooden fence along the edge of the parking lot, resting his thumbs in the pockets of his jeans.

"So. How've you been?"

I suspected his thoughts were on something other than the question as I joined him against the fence and faced out toward the hotel. I felt a strange relief standing near him, an absence of the needy pull I had experienced back then that had made me feel powerless whenever someone wanted something from me—even if it was something I was willing to give. I tossed the question back at him and noticed as he adjusted the crotch of his jeans. I couldn't help a tiny smile as I wondered if it was because of me.

Phillip turned around to look across the street with me. Deep blue was replacing the pink-orange shades of dusk in real-time increments. It would be dark in a matter of minutes.

"They plowed over our place," he said.

I almost laughed. "Yep."

And I had plowed over a lot of who I had been then. The poignancy of the realization probably showed on my face, and I was glad he wasn't looking at me.

Barely realizing it, we had left the fence and started across the pavement, none of the rush that used to attend our sneaking out there six years prior accompanying us. The street was unoccupied as we crossed it slowly, almost automatically, not stopping until we reached the far side of the hotel. There we stood, behind a new structure hidden in old shadows.

Phillip stepped toward me, his eyes darkening with an oh-so-familiar desire. "So what do you say?" His voice was low, tight with lust. "One more for old times' sake?"

This time I let the laugh out. "Old times' sake, Phillip?" The words came without hesitation, no part of me feeling unsure about what I said, what I was about to do. How he responded, of course, was up to him. "How about payback." I planted my hands on his shoulders and pushed him abruptly to his knees. Phillip blinked up at me in surprise, a response I ignored as I slid my skirt up and pulled my panties off to the side. My eyes stayed on his.

After a pause Phillip leaned forward, lifting his hands tentatively to my thighs as his warm breath joined the coolness of the night that surrounded my naked pussy. I sighed as his lips touched me, holding back a groan as his tongue slid its way over my clit. In short order I forgot anything but sensation as he delved into me, his earnestness rivaling that which I had shown him years before.

My casual air disappeared as I started to care what he did, the heat in my core eliciting a fervent hope that he wouldn't stop, that he'd finish this job as well as I had always finished it for him. Every nerve ending in my body fixated on little more than his tongue as I realized just how much power someone in his position really had.

He squeezed my ass hard as my body began to contract. I bit back a scream and came against his tongue, grabbing the back of his head and grinding against him with animalistic abandon.

A true reversal of roles.

I panted as I came back down, maintaining enough cognizance to drop my skirt and square my shoulders as he stood up.

"Thanks." I smiled and turned to leave, just like he had all those times after I'd given him what he wanted.

"Melissa."

I turned back. His demeanor was tentative and vulnerable, a tempered version of the thoughtless cockiness he'd embodied the summer I'd last seen him. I realized suddenly that he'd seen six years of experience since then too—and like his ignorance of mine, I had no idea what any of it was.

With a crooked smile, he said, "You'd need a couple dozen more to make it even."

I met his eyes. Something more than heat and desire lay behind the gaze that lingered on mine, and I realized he was saying he was sorry.

My lips pulled in another smile—involuntary this time. I shrugged, a gesture of acknowledgment, of agreement, of surprise and interest and assent. I gave him a nod as I pulled out my keys.

"Fair enough. See you tomorrow."

THE BEAST WITHIN (A MODERN-DAY FAIRY TALE)

In the headquarters of Castle Jewelers, the young CEO sat, as usual, locked away from everyone in his high tower office. He glared at the email from the Board of Directors open on his computer and the corresponding appointment notice on his calendar and snarled out loud as he turned his chair away and stood up. The CEO was a notorious figure among the employees that sat in the offices below him—his internal ugliness had become legendary, making his chosen reclusion in his office welcome among all who worked for him. The impeccability of his blue suit and expensive gold jewelry did nothing to hide the beastly disposition his workers had always seen in him.

Across town, Julie Bellevue had been called from her small cottage by the lake. Her father had fallen from his ladder as he was fixing the siding on his house and hurt his ankle. Julie hovered now by her father's hospital bed as the doctor informed them the ankle was broken.

Mr. Bellevue moaned. "Oh, what am I going to do? I have my first appointment with Castle Jewelers in an hour. I have to be there."

Julie, who was his youngest daughter, reached for his hand, her beautiful face drawn with sympathy. He turned to her.

"Julie, sweetheart, I'm going to need you to go and take over the job in my place."

Julie felt some apprehension at his request. The young woman was already an employee of her father's consulting business that specialized in conflict resolution for businesses and organizations. Though her father had been grooming her in his line of work for years, and she had recently acquired her master's degree in transpersonal psychology, she had not yet served as a lead with any client.

"Please, Julie. This is a very important client—I can't afford to lose it right now."

Julie recognized the desperation in his face, and she knew this job was an important one, both financially and for his reputation. If it were lost, the hard work he had put into forming and running his consulting business for the last several years could be in jeopardy.

So, to save her father's business, Julie agreed to take on her first client and go to Castle Jewelers headquarters in his place. As she started to take her leave, her father called her back.

"Julie," he said, concern evident on his face. "Your meeting is with the CEO—Heath Castle. The board has hired us to work with him individually in addressing the conflict between him and, well, the rest of the company. I was to coach him in sensitivity training and interpersonal communication.

"I want you to be warned—Heath is not said to be a nice individual. He has, in fact, an ugly reputation. He is said to be a rather beastly man and manager, very difficult to work with. His workers mostly vacillate between fear and loathing of him, and he's not usually seen around the workplace.

Generally, he locks himself in his office in the highest tower of the building."

"What makes him so not nice?" Julie asked.

Her father's expression twisted into a half smile as he shook his head. "That's what they pay us to find out."

AT THE HIGHEST office in the top of the headquarters building, Julie met the eyes of the company's thirty-eight-year-old CEO. She had been struck by the young age of the head of such a large and lucrative company as she'd read her father's file, and upon reading further, she had found that the circumstances surrounding his position were a bit mysterious—it was a family company, and Heath's mother had taken over after his father had died several years before. She had run the company for a short time before Heath had abruptly assumed the leadership role. There was no further information about his mother's current status with the company or why this turnover had taken place.

The man in front of her had a tall, sturdy, potentially intimidating build as he stood with his arms crossed behind his desk to greet her. His hair was dark and longish, his suit tailored to fit his bulky frame flawlessly. The truth was that Heath was a handsome man, but no one who worked for him even noticed his physical attractiveness anymore, so accustomed were they to the hideousness of his demeanor.

It was when Julie looked into the man's eyes that she saw what her father had warned her about. They appeared flat, dark with hostility, and emanated an energy about as welcoming as a prison. Heath in fact had eyes of a lovely bright blue, but they had reflected darkness for so long that they appeared simply black to most who looked at him now.

Julie's father had been retained to conduct a one-hour

session with Heath each morning for two weeks. As Julie began their first session, she understood immediately the complaints of those who worked for him and the reason the board had procured her father's services. The voice of the man in front of her was low and menacing, and not once while she was in his office did he smile. At times his demeanor was downright ferocious, almost animal-like in the refined environment of posh furniture and spectacular views from the broad window behind the desk. That day's meeting was the initial consultation, and Julie's heart sank a bit as she realized she would be trapped in this office tower with Heath every weekday morning for the next two weeks.

Like most people, the beautiful young woman also forgot about the attractiveness of Heath's physical appearance as she interacted with the internal ugliness that had so alienated his employees. Even so, when she stood up at the conclusion of their initial session, she found herself admiring his solid build and chiseled features, formed into a frown as frequently as they were. She leaned forward to shake his hand and bid him well for the day, and his eyebrows came together in an even deeper frown as he hesitated before offering her what may have been the coldest handshake she had ever experienced.

Each day when Julie came and went, she passed by Vivian, the receptionist, who had made no secret of the fact that she found Julie's job far from enviable.

"Good luck doing that kind of work with such a beast of a man," Vivian had said not unpleasantly when Julie had introduced herself her first day there. "He'd just as soon growl a nasty comment at you as say hi!"

As the week progressed, Julie smiled to herself when she recalled Vivian's obvious display of sympathy. To be sure, she found working with Heath distasteful sometimes, and at times she even grew frustrated, but Julie had been raised very consciously, and she knew that the only way to overpower hate was with love. Love could take many forms—kindness, protectiveness, fierceness—but it was essential in all dealings in order for them to retain the power of truth. So she took a deep breath and found that awareness in her heart, and whenever she responded to Heath, she did so from that place.

Though Julie was a clever girl and had discerned an understanding of many things about Heath thus far, she was unaware that an unwanted attraction he felt toward her was making him even edgier than usual. He had no desire to give in to any kind of connection with anyone, and the carnal pull inside him whenever the image of the enticing young woman floated across his consciousness was something he simply clenched his jaw against and pushed from his awareness as he had so many other things.

When she was physically present in his office, the challenge of that increased. One such time he even found himself remembering the single unopened condom he had tossed in the bottom drawer the morning he had discovered it mysteriously lying beneath his desk. (This was only mysterious to Heath because he was unaware of the pastime the cleaning crew enjoyed of having irreverent sex atop his desk after hours.) When he realized where his mind had drifted, he had slammed a fist onto his desk and said some vicious thing to the beautiful woman sitting on the other side of it. She had met his gaze, never losing her cool. Heath, on the other hand, had found himself shaking and clamped down with even greater resolve on the unwelcome libidinous urges that had crept their way into his experience.

On Monday morning of the second week, Julie entered the office in a bright yellow power suit with a lavish bouquet of red roses in her hands. Vivian looked up from her desk as Julie passed by with the large vase.

"Ooh!" the receptionist said, her eyes lighting up. "Who gave you flowers?"

Julie gave a tinkling laugh as she paused. "No one, Viv darling. I bought them myself."

Vivian's brow crinkled. "You bought roses for yourself?"

Julie laughed again. "They're for my father. Red is his favorite color. I'm taking them to him later to cheer him as he heals."

With a little wave she turned and continued down the row of cubicles to the elevators, and a smiling Vivian turned back to her desk. Though Julie had been headed to Heath's office carrying a bouquet of flowers, it never occurred to Vivian or any of the workers in any of the cubicles that the roses might be for him, as no one liked him enough to even consider that anyone would bring him something so nice.

Heath didn't look up as Julie sailed into his office, and she accepted this slight with her usual grace. At the soft sound of the glass vase lowering onto a shelf, his head lifted. He did a double take as his gaze landed on the flowers.

"What the hell are those?" he demanded, his gaze darkening even more than usual.

"Roses," Julie said, stating the obvious. "I'm taking them to my father's house on my way home."

Heath's glare had grown more pronounced as she spoke, even as it didn't leave the blooms now set atop the shelf. "I don't want them in here. Get rid of them!"

Julie looked at him evenly. "Heath, a little brightness in this room while I'm here is not going to hurt you."

Heath looked enraged, and he stood up, slamming his palms on the desk in front of him. "If you don't get them out of here, I'll do it myself."

He made a move from behind the desk, and Julie stepped calmly in front of him. Neither spoke for a moment as they stood toe to toe, Heath breathing heavily, Julie meeting his gaze with the silent strength she had always shown in the face of Heath's hostility. It was this time that she saw, as she looked into his stormy gaze, the flicker of sadness she suspected he didn't even consciously register. His aggression, his maleness, stood inches from her, and while she felt the stirring of arousal in her gut at the challenge, she took a deep breath and tempered it in the face of her immediate duty.

"What do you have against roses?" she ventured in a quiet voice.

The flicker grew then, but was quickly replaced by an even stronger fury. "I hate them," he snarled, moving to push past her, but Julie stayed rooted, and her steadfastness made Heath back up. He dropped into his chair with an angry thud.

The progress Julie had made working with Heath over the last week began to show when he chose to actually offer more information. In a low, furious voice, he muttered through clenched teeth, "They remind me of my mother."

"What?" Julie was surprised by the disclosure, and she stepped closer to him.

"Nothing." Just as quickly Heath retracted, and Julie felt his energy draw back in as his nostrils flared with anger.

"Would you like to tell me about your mother?" Julie's voice was quiet, the invitation like a feather floating through the air between them.

"My mother was an evil witch. It's because of her that I'm the way I am!" With this furious outburst, Heath stood and stalked to the window, sending his rolling chair flying back to bang against the wall.

Julie looked at him, sensing the importance of his words. "What way is that?"

Heath whirled on her and glared. "Do you think I don't know what people think about me? What they say? That no one wants me around? Why the fuck do you think I stay locked in my office all damn day? Because I like it so much?" He gave a dry laugh that scraped like metal against concrete. "Not quite, sweetheart. It's because I know people don't want me around. Which is fine, because I don't want to be around them, either."

Julie didn't answer, sensing, despite his anger, that she should let him continue. The young woman was surprised to find that his use of the word "sweetheart" had given the undeniable arousal in her a jolt. She took a deep breath, however, and released the distraction, focusing again on her present responsibility. She stood still and remained quiet, holding a place of safety for him to speak if he wanted to.

After a few minutes, his voice started up again. "I had a younger sister. Michelle. We grew up rich, of course. Materially, we had all we could ever want." His jaw clenched. "But my father worked all the time, and my mother—my mother hurled nothing but cruelty at my sister and me. We threatened to run away, but my mother told us we were ugly children, and that no one else would ever want us." He turned away from Julie, and she could see him trembling as he stared out the window.

"Michelle killed herself." The words were like the wretched creak of an abandoned, centuries-old castle door. "After that, my mother ran off. I never saw her again." He turned slowly from the window. Fury sparked from his eyes as he trained his seething gaze on the bouquet of roses on the shelf. "She sent a spray of red roses to Michelle's funeral, even though she knew Michelle hated red."

Julie remained silent, allowing Heath's words to land and be heard.

After several minutes, she spoke, barely above a whisper. "I'm so sorry about your sister." She paused, then went on. "And I can understand your feeling very hurt by your mother's actions."

Heath didn't move, though she saw his jaw clenching and unclenching.

"And it's because of that hurt that you've treated people so cruelly yourself." Julie said it as a statement, albeit a gentle one, rather than a question. In Heath's eyes she saw the understanding of the declaration as truth.

It encouraged her, and she spoke again. "What might that tell you about why your mother treated you so cruelly?"

"What?" he snapped.

She repeated herself, pausing to allow the question to register before adding, "I don't know what happened in her life or why she herself felt so much pain. But the bottom line is, it was likely the pain in her that hadn't been released that made her treat her children that way."

A look of sadness came over Heath like the sun from behind a cloud. "I know what happened to her." His expression became so distressed it looked as though he might cry. "She *was* hurting." Then his expression hardened. "But it wasn't fair for her to take that out on us."

Julie acknowledged his comment with an emphatic nod. "You're right, Heath. It isn't fair to take our pain out on others."

Her gaze stayed on him as he looked at her, the internal struggle smoldering in his expression. His eyes were dark again, and Julie could see he had not understood. The defensiveness was rising up in him, threatening to take over and burst through to an even stronger degree than before. Julie knew it was not unusual for defenses to arise in the face of revelation, and for the mental processing of words alone to not be enough. She saw the opportunity, and she knew she would need to take a different tack.

The pain, like a spell, needed to be broken.

Anger continued to rise visibly in Heath, and Julie took a deep breath, allowing fierce love, love in its warrior form, to rise inside her as it was called forth. When she felt it fill her being, she stepped forward and met the stony gaze of her client head-on, her own reflecting the hardness of twin diamonds.

"Sit down." Her voice had changed. She heard it, and she could tell by the look on Heath's face that he did too. Wariness among the fury and bitterness now, he hesitated only a second before lowering himself into his chair.

Julie reached forward and started to untie his tie. Her closeness made Heath's breath hitch even as he began to demand to know what she thought she was doing.

The sharp connection of her hand with his face resounded in the office before his sentence was even finished. Heath's jaw dropped, though the countenance of Julie, who happened to know how to deliver such a slap without actually damaging anything, didn't change.

"I'm doing whatever I want, and you will do so as well until I release you from that order." She pulled his tie the rest of the way off and stepped back. "Stand up." Julie minced no words as the orders came through her, the alignment of fierce love displaying its unique beauty.

Still stunned, Heath did so without a word. Julie turned him around and secured his wrists behind his back with his tie. She felt his muscles tense beneath her hands, and she left one hand on his arm after she was finished, sending warmth from her body into his via the physical contact. She kept it there until she felt a degree of relaxation beneath her fingers. Then she put a hand on his shoulder, bending him at the waist and pushing his cheek down to the surface of his desk.

Though Heath would never have wanted to admit it, Julie's sudden treatment of him seemed to make the arousal he had clamped down so tightly rocket into his consciousness like an erupting volcano, his cock providing immediate and granite-like evidence as such. He stayed still in the position she had put him in, desperately hoping she wouldn't notice this incriminating circumstance.

Then Julie was behind him, her body pressing against his as she leaned forward and grabbed his hair. Reaching below the desk, she grabbed his crotch without preamble. Heath jerked with humiliation, his face burning from being caught in such a state of arousal. Julie, on the other hand, almost breathed a sigh of relief. Though she had fully expected it, she was more than a little relieved to feel the hardness between his legs. Her instincts had been correct.

The revelation also made the wetness grow between her own legs. The arousal she had felt earlier was in full force now, but she still relegated it to a secondary position, inviting her slick pussy to be patient while she attended to the struggle taking place within Heath.

Julie held his hair unflinchingly and squeezed the base of his erection just hard enough to keep his attention.

"Do you like that?" she hissed in his ear, tightening the grip of both her hands. She let go of his cock and undid his belt as he whimpered incoherently. She yanked his trousers open unceremoniously, and they fell to the floor.

The smack resounded in the cavernous office as Julie brought her hand down against his right buttock. Heath jumped and cried out as Julie's hand, already poised for the second blow, found its left counterpart target before she paused and ran her hand over the red blossoming over his skin. She kept her grip on his hair, the warmth of her hand exuding a strength she knew was founded on compassion and alignment, whether or not Heath felt it consciously yet. Over and over she hit him, then caressed him, checking the surging of his cock periodically and barking orders as he squirmed beneath her hands. The energy swelled and retreated like an orchestra, the harmony and dissonance of hers and his and that which was unique to their connection administering just enough pain to touch what was repressed within him.

As it did, Julie watched as the immediate and past hurt melded together, rising into Heath's consciousness as his body shuddered and she held on tighter, holding steady and guiding him with her hands and her heart to release. To the place where what had been trapped for so long was experienced, processed in a moment of agony that for an instant seemed everlasting before it exploded and vanished, just another form of light in the infinite array of all that is. Julie caught her breath when Heath's cock finally erupted at the same time he did, his body collapsing in a roaring sob as his come spurted over her fingers.

Julie yanked the tie off his wrists and moved immediately to cover his body with hers, holding him tightly as he released beneath her. The energy affected her deeply, and she found herself feeling awash in the beauty that broke forth from beneath the beastliness that had covered it for who knew how long. The transformation took her breath away, transferring effortlessly through her body to the arousal spilling between her legs.

Seamlessly Julie slid her mouth to Heath's ear. Careful to only complement and not interrupt the long-overdue expression as it came from him, the words were barely a whisper, almost simply a movement against his skin:

"You're beautiful."

Heath's body convulsed, his sobs continuing long after his orgasm had culminated. Eventually he fell silent. Without a sound, Julie lifted her body slowly from his, watching as he took a deep breath and stood, his eyes still closed.

When he turned to her and opened them, Julie blinked at the transformation. She was startled to discover how blue Heath's eyes were, as though the tears had literally cleaned them out, polished away the tarnish to restore them to their original luster.

They were also, she noted, filled with desire, of a potency and purity she had not yet seen from him. Before she could respond, Heath stepped toward her and lifted her from the floor, almost crushing her in his embrace as he backed her up against the wall, his mouth on hers with a sizzling urgency that swept all professional considerations from her consciousness. Nothing but her sex commanded attention now, the dripping between her legs covering Heath's fingers as he slipped his hand beneath her yellow skirt.

Gently Heath lowered Julie to the wooden floor, unbuttoning her suit jacket and sliding her bra out of the way as he took one nipple and then the other into his mouth, eliciting in Julie a burning desire over which she felt no influence. Rising to his knees, Heath yanked open the bottom drawer of his desk and scrabbled through it frantically until he found the tiny foil packet he had remembered only days before.

Then he sank into Julie, who was waiting beneath him with flushed face and rapid breath. The two of them cried out in unison as he entered her, and her arms came around his strong shoulders as he moved his hips with exquisite slowness. Julie's breath grew even faster as Heath felt her start to tremble beneath him.

When her release came, she wailed with abandon, releasing all the earnestness she had collected while caring for Heath and succumbing to her own state of sublimity. They lay on the floor together, neither speaking nor moving, for some time. When Julie eventually rose and began to straighten her outfit, Heath stood up as well.

"I'll walk you downstairs," he said. For the first time, Julie saw him smile.

Moments later the two stood just inside the glass door in the entryway of Castle Jewelers headquarters as their lips came together in a kiss softer than the rose petals adorning the stems Julie held. Behind them, Vivian's eyes nearly sprang from their sockets as she stared unabashedly from her desk.

As they eased apart, Julie extracted, with exquisite delicacy, one of the scarlet blooms from the vase. With reverence, she extended it gently to the man in front of her.

Heath swallowed and looked down at the flower before lifting his big hand to accept it.

"Please don't tell me I must wait until tomorrow to see you again," he whispered as he looked back up at her.

Julie smiled. "I'll text you my address right now." Palming her phone from her purse, she gave Heath a last kiss on the cheek and strode through the glass door into the sunlight beyond.

And so it was that the beast within was released in the face of unconditional love. Because Julie had loved and accepted even what was ugly in Heath, it had transformed and returned to the beauty inherent in all things. From that day forth, Heath became beautiful again to all who knew him, and especially to Julie, who continued to visit his tower office long after their two-week contract was up whenever he wasn't already taking the day off to spend at her small cottage by the lake.

WHO'S ON TOP?

"Got a game in your head?"

They were the first words Corey ever said to me, startling me as he approached from behind. I was standing in my neighborhood park, gazing at the silent baseball field in front of me. It was a simple field, situated in the far corner of the park off the soccer field. It didn't have dugouts or bleachers, just a single metal bench for each team behind a chain-link fence that bordered the home plate corner.

But as simple as it was, a baseball field was a baseball field as far as I was concerned. A Yankees fan from birth, I grew up in New York City with baseball literally in my blood: my parents met each other at Yankee Stadium during game six of the 1977 World Series. Having moved away from home but stayed on the East Coast, I still went home for a game several times a season, but for the most part, I had to make do now watching them on TV.

In the meantime, I liked to visit the simple field whenever I found myself at the park. My favorite time to come was at dusk, when the no-use-after-dark rule of the park was just about to take effect and parents were starting to gather their little ones and hurry home. I'd sit on the benches, wander the baselines, and lean against the chain-link fence behind home plate, appreciating whatever it was that attracted me about an empty playing field at night.

It was there I stood that evening mid-season, fingers laced through the metal as I watched the sun disappear behind second base, when I jumped at those words: *Got a game in your head?*

Turning, I saw an intriguingly hot stranger walking toward me, his hands in his jeans pockets.

"Sorry, I didn't mean to startle you. I'm Corey."

"Paige," I said, stepping away from the fence to shake his hand. Glancing back at the field, I smiled and said, "I was just having a solitary moment of baseball appreciation."

Corey laughed. "Yeah, I know what you mean."

And he did, I could tell. I met his dark-brown eyes and felt heat stirring in me as I looked him up and down. He joined me at the fence, and we turned back toward the field as darkness fell. I didn't know it yet, but what attracted me about an empty playing field at night was about to get a whole lot more involved.

***

WE EXCHANGED NUMBERS, but as it turned out, neither of us had a chance to use them before we ran into each other the next day in the exact same place. I didn't usually find myself at the park so early in the afternoon, but I had decided to watch the community youth coed baseball game, and as I strolled up to the field, I caught sight of Corey. He stood beside one of the team's benches, his arms crossed in the unmistakable stance of a coach.

Surprised by the coincidence, I started toward him.

Before I reached him, he turned his head, and I saw the red "B" on his hat. I stopped.

He was a Red Sox fan.

At that moment he caught sight of me, and his face lit up when his eyes met mine—until they dropped slightly to my jacket.

I was wearing my Yankees pullover, and his expression immediately shifted to one of surprise and then distaste.

As much as I was a Yankees fan through and through, I didn't get into team rivalries as much as some, appreciating the game itself more than particular team competitions. Nonetheless, I was sure we were both aware that our respective teams happened to be facing off that very night with the first of a three-game series in New York. Even as I felt the heat rise in me, I held my smile in check, not knowing how seriously Corey took the biggest rivalry in baseball.

His hard gaze stayed on mine. I held it.

The inning of the game in front of us ended, and his team started to filter back behind the fence to the bench he stood beside. I gave a final nod, my smile just starting to appear as I turned on my heel. The question would be answered, I supposed, by whether or not I ever heard from him again.

Either way, my team had better win that night.

───

My phone rang as I pulled a carton of ice cream from the freezer that evening.

"Gearing up to watch your team get its ass kicked?" Corey said without preamble.

A ping of arousal shot through me, and I smiled wryly. "Indeed I am getting ready to watch my team," I said, "though I certainly bank on a different outcome. Is there something I can do for you?"

"I was thinking maybe we could watch the game together."

My eyebrows rose. "You don't mind having a gloating Yankees fan by your side for nine innings?" Gloating wasn't my style, but he didn't know that, and I was curious how he would respond.

"Not when she doesn't have anything to gloat about," Corey countered.

My eyes narrowed despite the smile that stayed in place. "You're on."

⁂

THE DOORBELL RANG just as the national anthem was coming to a close. I opened the door to find Corey standing on the threshold, the same cap on his head and a knowing grin on his face. Another jolt of arousal shot through me at the sight of him, stronger this time—and laced with the dark streak of challenge.

I stepped back to let him in. He moved forward and kissed me without pretense. My breath caught, and I kissed him back and felt both of us tense, ready to push the other against the wall. The result was a split-second wrestling match; breathless, we broke apart and laughed.

"So," I said. "You're a Red Sox fan."

"All my life." He grinned and moved past me as I shut the door.

I gestured toward the couch and followed him to it. "Can I get you anything?"

His eyes flicked quickly up and down me. "No thanks," he answered as he settled on the couch. I sat down beside him, and he turned to me. "So. I've never had sex with a Yankees fan before."

I quirked an eyebrow. "Gee, Corey, should I take that as an indication that you think we're going to have sex?"

He laughed. "Something about the look you managed to give me today even in your contempt at realizing I was a Sox fan made me think that was maybe on your mind."

I smirked, not bothering to refute what was true. Turning to the TV screen, I took in the scene of the familiar stadium where I'd seen the same matchup in person many times. The energy of the raw love of baseball filled me, along with the suspense I felt whenever I watched the Yankees play. I gave Corey a sidelong glance as I felt the charge in the room increase. I did want us to win.

Corey turned to me. "Interested in making a little bet on this game?"

The gleam in his eye made me have to actively hold back from jumping on him. "What kind of bet?"

He leaned in a little closer. "Winner gets to have his—or her—way with the loser, so to speak."

"What?"

"Winner gets to dominate," he explained.

I blinked. After that instant of surprise, I dropped my eyes as I realized immediately what a twist that would present for me, though he was not aware of it. I glanced down at his hand, extended toward me to shake on the deal. After a moment I slipped mine into it. We both grasped firmly, our eyes hard.

Born and raised in New York, I came from a family of unambiguous, die-hard Yankee fans. I'd lived and breathed the Yankees ever since I was old enough to know what they were. Rooting for my team was second nature to me, and it went without saying that I wanted them to win. Always.

But I also loved to be dominated.

TWO NIGHTS LATER, I carried a bottle of red wine to the coffee table and set the glasses on coasters. A knock on the door came as I headed back to the kitchen. I stopped to open it, and Corey entered with a grin and shut the door behind him.

As we made our way to the sofa, we both affected a casual countenance, pretending to ignore the fact that this was the night of nights for our little game. I had to admit that it had been throwing my lifelong team loyalty into turmoil, the unquestioned nature of it colliding and conflicting with the simple desire to be thrown/pushed/held/tied down and fucked hard.

Tonight was the third and final game of this Red Sox/Yankees series. I had been relegated to being Corey's sexual submissive for the hour after the first game ended two nights before, and even now I grew wet as I recalled the way he pushed me to my knees and grabbed the back of my head as he shoved his cock down my throat.

Last night had brought a switch in my favor when the Yankees had pummeled the Red Sox nine to one. I didn't usually prefer sexual dominance, but there was no question Corey was getting off on it as I shoved him face-down over the back of the couch and smacked his ass until it was bright red, putting the paddle he had used on me to my own extensive use....

"Here you go." Corey's voice snapped me back to the present as he finished pouring and handed me my wine glass. I took a deep breath, wet from my reminiscences. In my head I knew I wanted the Yankees to win tonight—as always. An uncontrollable intensity in my body, however, pulled insistently at the desire to be held down and fucked hard under utter submission.

I tried to sit still on the couch, but the unpredictable nature of our little game was becoming almost unbearably frustrating. I just wanted to fuck. Corey sat down beside me, and I knew I wasn't going to last the whole game. The Red Sox were up; as their batter slid safely into second, Corey turned to me with that gleam in his eye and grabbed my hair, pulling me in for a hard kiss.

"Are you suggesting we go play by play tonight?" I asked a little breathlessly when he pulled away.

"Maybe inning by inning." He grinned.

I couldn't remember another game when I'd looked forward to the commercial breaks.

"Walk this way," Corey said as he grabbed his keys and headed toward the door.

"Where are we going?" I couldn't resist asking, surprised. The Red Sox victory was his cue to lead me to whichever room he chose and do what he would with me. The thought made me shiver even as I cast one last glare at the final score before pressing the power button on the remote.

Apparently he wasn't choosing a room this time. "That's for me to know," he said as we headed outside.

He opened his passenger door for me, and we drove in silence. A slow smile spread across my face as he pulled up along the curb by the park where we'd met. I knew he had avoided the parking lot so as not to arouse suspicion, as the park was closed after dark. Having been in this park at night many times, I was aware that the cops usually did a single obligatory drive through at about 1:00 a.m. That being hours away, I certainly hoped tonight wouldn't be an exception.

I followed Corey through the darkness, our feet rustling the lush grass beneath us. It was so quiet I could hear my breathing. As we approached the chain-link fence where we'd met, he cut around past one of the dugout benches and walked onto the field. He led me to home plate and stopped.

Dropping on the ground a small bag I had seen him grab from his backseat, he kissed me hard before pushing me to my knees on the gravel.

"Don't move," he ordered as he reached for the bag. He pulled a rope of some sort out of it and moved behind me. I felt my wrists being grabbed and tied together behind my back.

Moving back in front of me, Corey stood on home plate as he freed his cock with one hand and grabbed a fistful of my hair with the other. The smell of the freshly mown field wafted around us, and I breathed it in heavily as I looked up at him, stars slathered across the black background above him.

He ran a finger along my jawline, slowly, gently, as I shifted from knee to knee on the sandy gravel. It dug into my skin, but my arousal was too overt for me to care. I was wet and fidgety as he held my head away from him, my mouth almost watering for the taste of his cock.

He slipped his finger lightly into my mouth, still holding my hair solidly to keep me from diving forward onto his cock like I wanted to. I looked up at him again, and when I met his eyes, I knew that he knew exactly what effect this was having on me. He pulled his hand away and positioned it back on his cock. Slowly, he stroked himself, holding my head and not letting me move.

I had never wanted a cock in my mouth so badly. Finally Corey reached under my chin and turned my face upward, making me meet his eyes.

"You ready to suck this cock?"

Yes flew from my mouth before I even had time to think about it. He continued to look at me. "Yes, please," I continued, the pleading in my voice real. He looked at me for another moment before putting his free hand on the back of my head and shoving my face forward with the force of both hands, pushing his cock deep into my throat. I almost gagged, but I had anticipated enough that I had time to breathe correctly. It was fortunate that I knew a thing or two about giving head—even by pseudo-force.

He held me in position for a few seconds before letting off and fucking my face rhythmically. The gravel was still biting into my knees, the ropes binding my wrists chafing slightly as I shifted my hands. Corey's hard length penetrated my lips repeatedly, banging against the back of my throat as my pussy got wetter by the second. Finally he yanked my hair back and pulled my head off his cock.

I looked up at him, his eyes like solid dark chocolate as he pulled me by my hair to my feet. Reaching behind me, he untied the rope holding my wrists and pushed me back up against the fence before reaching again for the bag lying nearby. He pulled out two more ropes, identical to the first.

"Spread your legs."

I did so, and he proceeded to tie each of my ankles to the fence. When he was done, he stood and attended to my wrists, lifting them over my head and binding them to the chain-link as well. When he stepped back, I was firmly bound by all four limbs to the fence behind home plate.

Corey hitched my denim skirt up to my waist. I had nothing on underneath, and I was sure he could see how wet I was just by looking. He seemed pleased as he stared between my legs.

"Do you like this? You like what I'm doing to you, baby?" he taunted, brushing his fingers over my vulva. I gasped and couldn't keep from crying out just a little. Immediately I bit my lip.

"I didn't think I'd have to tell you to be quiet here, Paige. Are you going to be a good girl, or do you need a gag?"

I shook my head. "No. I'll be good."

"You'd better. Another sound and I'll make it so you can't make any more."

Corey leaned in and ran his tongue across my lips, pulling back slightly whenever I tried to meet his mouth and kiss him. I squirmed in frustration.

Abruptly I felt his finger enter me; I hadn't known it was anywhere near me. I shrieked quietly, wincing as I realized I'd just broken the rules.

"Uh-huh," Corey said shortly, backing off and returning to the bag. "I see you're having some trouble following the rules tonight." He wasn't smiling as he pulled a ball gag from the bag.

"I didn't mean to. I won't do it again," I pleaded as he advanced toward me with the gag. I submitted sorrowfully as he installed it in my mouth, reminding me in a murmur of our safe symbol we'd agreed to use in lieu of the ability to say the safe word.

He yanked open the buttons on my shirt and popped the front clasp of my bra. The warm night breeze graced my breasts, but I shivered as Corey traced a finger along each of my nipples, watching them get hard. Then he grabbed me roughly, my pussy going into overdrive as he squeezed my tits in his fists.

He drew back and pulled a condom from the pocket of his jeans. His eyes were hard, forming mine into soft pools of submission as I breathed heavily, my tits exposed to the night, skirt at my waist, wrists bound above me, and ropes around my ankles holding my legs spread wide.

Corey moved back toward me and grasped my throat, pushing my head back against the hard chain-link. I felt the wetness between my legs start to drip.

With a grunt, he pushed into me, still gripping me in a choke hold, his other hand laced through the chain-link near my head. He pumped hard, eventually grasping my hips with both hands for better traction as I moaned as much as I could through the gag. It was good that it was there, it occurred to me, so my screams weren't heard by the quiet households surrounding us, most fast asleep by now.

Corey came in me with a hiss, then pulled out and looked me up and down. He backed up, removing the condom and zipping up his jeans, and focused on my throbbing clit. Stepping forward, he removed the gag from my mouth.

"I want to hear you call my name in my ear when you come. But not too loud—we don't want to wake up the nice suburban neighbors."

He reached for my clit and gently ran his finger across it.

"Oh," I gasped, urgency taking my breath away. I pulled at the restraints on my wrists, desperately wanting to touch myself along with him. He noticed and smiled.

"Sorry, doll, this is my game, remember? You lost tonight. Your hands will stay where I put them until I say so."

His voice and his words, taunting me, made me squirm under his ever-rougher touch. The release in me was building, and there was nothing left for me to do but give in, relinquish all control inside myself; outside, I already had none.

"Come for me—now. Now, Paige." Corey's voice got rough, and I screamed full force as my body exploded, Corey's hand moving immediately to cover my mouth and muffle the sound. The restraints holding my limbs suddenly served to protect me from gravity as every nerve in my body let go, swept by the orgasm that consumed them. The fence jangled and swished behind me, the reverberation rippling to the top of the chain-link like an extension of the orgasmic waves ripping through my body.

When it was over, I hung limply, trying to catch my breath, tiny breathless sobs forced out of me by pure intensity. Corey smiled and moved in to kiss me, softly this time, as he reached up to untie my wrists. When that was done, he attended carefully to my ankles, dropping the restraints one by one back into the bag. He pulled me gently to him, arms around my waist, and I rested my head against his shoulder for a moment and inhaled deeply.

We walked without speaking back across the grass. Corey placed his hand lightly on the small of my back as we reached the car, as though we were a couple greeting the valet after a lovely dinner instead of two people who barely knew each other who had just engaged in bondage sex in a park after hours. I smiled and brushed some of the dirt from my knees before settling into the passenger seat.

Back at my house, Corey left the bag in the car, and we entered through the front door. I retrieved my own carefully packed bag that I had set out in anticipation and returned it to the closet. Corey noticed.

"And what's that?" he asked, seeming genuinely surprised.

I glanced back at him. "You think you're the only one who knows the art of preparation?" I closed the closet door, picturing the brand-new strap-on dildo tucked away in the bottom of my bag. "Don't forget, Corey dear, we've still got half a season left. You may have gotten lucky tonight—but I think we both know who's going to come out on top."

WINTER

The temperature gauge on the rental car registered nineteen degrees. Unused to the absence of streetlights, signs, and other indicators of human life, Sherry kept her eyes on the highway and the snow lining either side of it; blackness dominated everything beyond the reach of the high beams. She had expected to feel lonely here, but inexplicably, Sherry found herself feeling less isolated than she often had for the last year and a half at home. The recognition was slightly unsettling.

"Why would you go to Alaska in the middle of winter?" one of her colleagues had asked at the staff meeting the day before. Sherry smiled wryly at the recollection. The question was predictable, but she hadn't been sure exactly how to answer it.

Glancing down at the directions she'd printed out before leaving that morning, Sherry noted a rare road sign and made the turn. The printout was a security measure, as she had been unsure what cell phone reception would be like during the hour-long drive between the Anchorage airport and the wilderness lodge where she was headed. She had been glad to find the remote resort open this time of year—it hadn't taken much research to find that many of them closed during the off-season.

Which brought her back to her coworker's question.

Sherry had seen an acupuncturist years before who told her that winter was the season of stillness, silence, depth, mystery. That energy and insights didn't surge forth in winter—that was the "upward and outward" offering of spring. Winter was a time of quiet; little movement; respecting the cold, dark, uninviting conditions and taking the opportunity to store and replenish one's internal energy in response. It was a notion Sherry had been skeptical of, even scoffed at, finding the idea of sitting around being still a waste of time.

There was nothing still or quiet indeed about nonprofit advocacy in Washington, DC—especially when it was political. Her position as the research director of an organization squarely in the political fray not only held the demands any such job would but also came with an opposition force whose goal was to obliterate everything she and her organization worked for.

But when the acupuncturist's words had come back to her on the heels of a holiday season wracked with memories of pain and betrayal, Sherry had experienced them differently for some reason. Granted, the notion of a three-day stay somewhere not only freezing but also generally deserted seemed a strange motivation to spend literally an entire day traveling. But Sherry had sensed that if she sought out somewhere warm, where things didn't need to slow down and she could flee the factors that nurtured the depth and quietness of winter in the first place, she would be inclined to avoid the season even more than she usually did and perhaps forget it altogether. Somehow, that suddenly seemed important.

With a last glance at the paper next to her, Sherry turned

into the parking area of the lodge and hauled her luggage up to the solid wooden door.

The warmth when she pulled it open was immediate and encompassing. On the left, the large open dining room was empty and immaculate, with buffet tables lining the opposite wall. On the right, floor-to-ceiling windows graced the far wall of the sizable but cozy lounge, which culminated in a stone fireplace centered on the wall she faced. Beyond that wall and to the left was the reception area, visible over the half wall topped by lacquered, log-like pillars that separated it from the dining area. A series of flat, forest-green rugs made a path on the wooden floor from the door past the fireplace to the front desk.

Lulled by the solitariness of her drive, Sherry was almost startled by the rumble of voices that had greeted her ears when she'd stepped through the door. She registered a group of five men gathered in armchairs near the lounge fireplace. They had all turned to her, and blushing a bit, Sherry returned their smiles as she started up the path of green rugs.

"Ms. Nielson?" The young man at the counter greeted her, and Sherry nodded.

"Welcome. I'm Kevin. My parents own the lodge, and I take care of the front desk and reservations during the off-season. You're one of only two parties here this weekend, and you just passed the other one on your way in."

He handed her a packet. "Here's your room key, as well as some information about area attractions and activities in the winter. It's well below freezing now, but it's supposed to get unusually warm—up to thirty-four degrees—starting Saturday and through the weekend.

"Your room is down that hall, to the right and then around the corner again, on the ground floor. It has a private deck with its own outside entrance and looks out the back of the building, toward the river."

"Thank you. That sounds lovely," Sherry spoke for the first time during Kevin's monologue, which he was obviously used to offering.

"Marina will be on-site to cook as requested, so please let me know if we can accommodate you for any meals. Your room also has a kitchenette, of course, and I see you brought groceries. Yes, Mr. Wyatt?"

Kevin had looked over her shoulder as he spoke the last sentence, and Sherry turned to see one of the men from the lounge approaching the desk. He was classically handsome, probably in his mid-forties, and wore a burgundy sweater that complemented his dark-brown hair.

"Excuse me," he said as he gave Sherry a friendly—and very attractive, she couldn't help noticing—smile before turning to Kevin with some question about freezer storage. Flustered, Sherry started to gather her things.

"Can I help you with that?" the man asked, turning his dark eyes to her as she finished juggling her backpack, suitcase, purse, and the bags of groceries she'd picked up in Anchorage.

"Oh, no, that's okay," she said hastily. Glancing down, she noticed without even meaning to the absence of a ring on his left hand. Despite the mysterious jolt the realization evoked, Sherry resisted the idea of social engagement in this place intended for stillness and silence. "Thank you."

She managed a quick smile and excused herself, glancing up once to meet his warm eyes again before swiveling and wheeling her suitcase behind her down the carpeted hall. Her heartbeat had almost returned to normal by the time she reached her door.

THE NEXT MORNING, Sherry curled up with a mug of tea on

the love seat in her suite. Though it was after 9:00, it was still dark out the back window, with blue hints of dawn just starting to appear among the birch trees. She could just barely make out the silhouette of the mountains on the other side of the river.

With nowhere she needed to go, Sherry continued to watch as pale pink seeped over the mountains. Soon bright orange seared a line above them, gradually taking over the tentative dark-blue sky as though night was being peeled off like a safety seal, slow and steady to keep the container from jerking and inadvertently spilling. Calm. Gentle. Careful.

A year and a half before, their daughter Jaci had just left for her first year of college in Connecticut when Sherry and her husband's marriage imploded. Abruptly, Sherry had found herself not only without the companionship of her daughter but without anyone at all—living alone for the first time in her life at age forty-three. She sipped her tea now and felt a deep hollowness in her belly. It was a sensation she'd experienced numerous times since her and Tom's sudden separation, especially during her hours in the severe emptiness of a house that used to hold those she loved most. Usually, no matter where she was, she managed to turn her focus to researching a bill or checking a news report or drafting a summary enough to quash the searing anguish into a dull ache that she covered with a thick layer of overwork.

Sherry's pulse sped up, drawing attention to the part of herself that feared that the isolation of Alaska would give free rein to this feeling that threatened to devour her alive. She took a breath and reminded herself what the acupuncturist had said those many years ago. Winter had something to offer. Sherry didn't know what it was, and maybe she never would, but she knew the very notion of stillness, of not doing anything, was foreign to her, especially since the divorce. And she couldn't deny that something felt more and more like it was disappearing into an abyss inside of her, and it was something that held in it the capacity to find joy in life. Somehow, the two seemed related.

Light continued to titrate the world outside the window, making the frost covering the glass both more visible and more hindering to the view beyond it. Sherry got up and moved closer to examine the frozen particles. Rather than the minuscule, nondescript specks of frost she was familiar with, these looked like tiny, elaborate frozen feathers. Fascinated, she wrapped her down parka around her and slipped into her waterproof boots before opening the back door and stepping onto the deck.

A frost from what seemed like another dimension covered every surface as far as she could see. Far from the dulling equivalent back home that simply indicated that it was cold, this frost glittered in the strengthening light, as though the particles were capturing the sun and smashing it into prismatic confetti before throwing it back into the icy air. The entire landscape looked like it was draped in sparkling frozen lace.

"Hoarfrost," Kevin said when she stopped by the front desk. "It happens during winter cold snaps here, which we've had throughout this week."

After getting directions from him to a relatively nearby glacier park, Sherry filled her backpack and started the drive, hoarfrost continuing to dominate the scenery around her in the white winter sunlight. Parking amid a surprising number of vehicles, Sherry stepped out to a view of towering mountains surrounding the water, their giant, jagged crevices looking like a network of intricate folds and creases from where she stood.

Much closer, the mammoth glacier stood like a frozen goddess of nature at the edge of the hard blue water. Since it was covered in snow, the breathtaking appearance of chiseled turquoise glass she'd seen in summer pictures was missing, but that did nothing to diminish the simple massiveness of the millennia-old structure that moved with exquisite slowness but carved the very earth in its wake. Its power was unmistakable.

In the water in front of her, icebergs of innumerable shapes and inconceivable proportions floated easily, as though they had put themselves on display just for the gratification of enthralled gazes like hers. Reminiscent of frozen clouds, they glowed with mysterious hues of deep blue, offering answers to questions long since lost to the icy waters beneath them. A bald eagle soared over the lake and landed on a misshapen block of ice not fifty yards away. The bird's talons curled sharply to dig into the ice as it settled in profile view and stared straight ahead. Its white head, precisely the same shade as the top of the iceberg, gleamed against the mountainous background.

Though she didn't move, Sherry had the distinct sensation of something inside her beginning to fissure, cracking open like the colossal sheets of ice that made up the land she stood upon. As the layer of distractions that dictated her day-to-day awareness started to dissolve, Sherry felt warily unaware whether that was desirable or not. She hoisted her backpack and started to hike, each step further illuminating the mystery of this land that was beyond anything a life of pressure and noise could hope to touch.

***

WHEN SHERRY EMERGED from the hallway into the front desk area Saturday morning, her five lodge-mates were in full view at a large table on the other side of the half wall. Her face reddened as she realized she was not going to get away with avoiding talking to them much longer. The one that had spoken to her at the desk Thursday night—Mr. Wyatt, Kevin had called him—had his back to her. Today he was in a navy-blue fleece.

The group was just starting to stand, and Sherry noticed the dishes on the table and deduced they had just finished breakfast.

"Good morning," she said quietly as a few of them caught sight of her when she entered the dining area. The one in the navy fleece turned, and she caught her breath as he met her eyes. Breaking into the easy smile he'd given her at the front desk, he stepped forward and offered his hand.

"Hi. I'm Dan," he said. "This is Larry, Stuart, Brett, and Kelsey." He indicated each of the others in turn as she shook their hands, immediately forgetting which was which.

"Sherry," she said, standing somewhat awkwardly as the group started to gather the outerwear they had set on nearby chairs.

"It's a pleasure to meet you, Sherry." Dan's brown eyes held hers. Up close, he appeared a few years older than she had originally thought, perhaps nearing fifty. His thick, dark-brown hair was edged with gray, and his face showed a comfortable maturity.

"What brings you to Alaska, Sherry?" the one that might have been Larry asked as he shrugged into a heavy black parka.

Sherry took a breath. She didn't feel much more inclined to have this conversation with the current group than she had with her coworkers earlier in the week. "I…was just looking for a place to retreat for a few days and basically relax," she said, her cheeks reddening a little. "In fact, I hope I haven't seemed rude not talking to you before now…. I just didn't really come to socialize."

Somewhat to her surprise, the group nodded as if in understanding, and she felt as though they actually did.

"Is this your first time in Alaska?" Dan asked.

"Yes…I have a feeling it's not yours?"

"We've all been to Alaska a number of times, though this is the first time we've managed to come as a group for a few years. We're from Vancouver. Brett and Stuart are brothers, and the rest of us have known each other for decades."

"Far too long," possibly Kelsey grunted, and Sherry smiled. She was enjoying their brief interaction more than she'd expected to. Something was missing here: a sharpness, a facade, some edge or something she didn't even usually identify because she was so used to it. It made interacting with people noticeably more enjoyable.

"Well, don't hesitate to let us know if you need anything or just want company for a while. We know this area pretty well." Dan flashed his disarming smile at her, and Sherry tried to ignore the fluttering in her stomach. His sincerity was downright refreshing—almost enchanting, actually.

"Thank you," she said, and she meant it. "It was a pleasure meeting you all," she said to the larger group as they returned the sentiment and ambled to the green rugs. Dan glanced back once and gave her a wave before they filed through the door out into the mid-morning darkness.

She poured herself coffee from the station at one of the buffet tables and sat near the table her lodge-mates had just vacated. She hadn't dated at all since her and Tom's separation. Usually it was something she neither thought about nor missed. She was surprised by the sensation she felt now in her sex, asking for attention in a way it hadn't in some time. Sherry didn't even recall the last time she had made herself come—which, she acknowledged grudgingly to herself, probably meant it had been a little too long.

That afternoon, she donned a white camisole, thermal

undershirt, light-gray wool turtleneck, and her gray fleece-lined leggings, followed by the new insulated "snow skirt" she had purchased for this trip. After pulling on her boots, she slipped her white ski band over her blond ponytail and stepped through the door onto her deck.

As she headed down to the river for a hike, she saw a set of tracks in the snow. Stopping, she studied them with an utter amateur's eye. From what she had read about animal tracks in this area, they appeared to be from a moose—surprisingly large, spread out due to the animal's long strides, and hoof-like. When she looked more closely at one, she saw the two telltale toe tracks—dewclaws, if she recalled correctly—of the moose's hoof.

With a strange sense of poignancy, Sherry straightened and looked out at the river, registering the wildness she had known existed on this planet but had never fully appreciated. The river and the atmosphere were still, and there was no sound on the frigid air surrounding her. Which did not mean, she was coming to understand, that nothing was happening. Amid this deep quiet, the unmoving surface of the water, a natural network of beings hunted, tracked, dug, foraged, observed, stored…existed. They conserved energy as they needed to and navigated winter with instinctual efficiency and brilliance.

The rain startled her. Sherry looked up and saw the gray cloud cover she somehow hadn't noticed juxtaposed with the light that still loomed over the distant mountains. The drops tapped like icy fingers on her shoulders as she breathed deeply and let the chill penetrate her in a way that was not unpleasant but rather, she suddenly noticed, made her feel more alive. The sheer rawness of it was riveting; an inexplicable exhilaration took her breath away.

When her clothes were soaked, she turned and started the short distance back to the lodge. Her body seemed mysteriously in collaboration with rather than resistant to the environment, and she didn't even pull her fleece from her backpack as she made her way through the now-slushy snow toward the outside entrance to her room.

As she neared the building, she noticed movement through a second-floor balcony door several rooms down from hers. Recognizing Dan and his fellow travelers standing just inside it, she looked away quickly, her cheeks heating. She was suddenly keenly aware of her hardened nipples beneath her wool turtleneck. While she felt a characteristic urge to cover or hide herself, another part of her felt something quite different—something that made her straighten her back imperceptibly, allowing her breasts to be in full view of any potential gazes through the glass. Her breath deepened as she imagined their private stares.

The rain continued to pelt her as something internal returned to chastise her for her silliness: they probably hadn't even noticed her. She risked another glance at the glass. Dan and two of the others lifted their hands in a wave, and Sherry almost jumped. Automatically she waved back before nearly sprinting across the deck to her door.

Well, of course they would wave, she realized as she peeled off her freezing leggings. They happened to be standing at their balcony door, and she happened to be walking by. It didn't mean they had seen her as closely as something in her seemed to want them to have.

Still, she found her fingertips brushing slowly over her breasts as she pulled her camisole over her head and turned on the shower. A current of heat sizzled through her as she imagined Dan's hands in place of her own. Drawing a breath, she maneuvered herself under the welcome stream of hot water and reminded herself that, while considerable, the privacy here was not complete whenever she stepped out of this room.

Kevin had generously given Sherry a late checkout time on Sunday, as she didn't need to be at the airport until evening for her overnight travels back to DC. After she'd finished packing, she pulled on what had become the standard amount of layers, slid into her boots, and headed out the back door with her backpack and sunglasses.

She walked for several minutes along the river, getting considerably further than she had the day before when the rain had tabled her hiking plans. When she was well beyond sight and earshot of the lodge, she sat down for one last opportunity to take in the silence and stillness of winter on this frozen Alaskan riverside.

The lack of wind made the cold seem almost neutral as her body felt as though it was sinking, drawn magnetically by the substance of the earth. The gentle force seemed to pull tension right out of her as she gazed at the impenetrable mountains that seemed to both split and simultaneously hold together the dull blue shade of the sky and water. Using her backpack as a pillow, Sherry lay back on the crusted snow.

The frozen ground beneath her felt solid and vital as the late-afternoon dusk colored the sky with a panoply of pastel purples, pinks, and blues. She couldn't remember ever feeling more solitary than she did at that moment, but there was nothing disquieting about the sensation. On the contrary, if she'd had to choose one word to describe what she felt right then, it would be "connected."

Then she felt it: the vast, infinite depth of stillness itself inside her. It was an unfamiliar sensation that reflected not only what she saw around her but what she instantly knew had been there all the time, unseen like whatever was beneath the motionless water mere feet away. It was the place from which slow, calm, muted offerings appeared, perfectly content to be where they were, as they were neither designed nor inclined to travel, but rather discoverable only within the stillness in which they dwelled.

This was what truly moved in winter. Only that which came from this true depth, whispering up like a pale reflection on rippling water, floating quietly to consciousness and landing with no fanfare, no effort, simply appearing. It didn't draw attention because it didn't need to. It was there for those who stopped and looked into the depth of the unseen, easily mistaken for a void of life and dynamism. But upon examination, so very clearly not.

Sherry felt her hand move almost involuntarily toward her pussy. Surprised, she started to stop herself. *You're in a public place!* something inside her screamed. But she was well out of view of the lodge, and the same part of her that had reveled in the saucy display of her hardened nipples the day before washed over her with the effortlessness of water, leading her to pull off her gloves and slide her fingers between her legs and stroke slowly, silently, over the soft fabric of her leggings. Surrender to it was as natural, as elemental, as the flight of the eagle she'd seen two days before.

Gathering her new snow skirt, she lifted the front of it to her waist and slid her leggings down to the tops of her boots. The still, freezing air felt crisp on her sex, and she bent her knees and spread her legs as wide as she could with her leggings still on.

She traced her wetness with an absence of urgency that seemed to be coming from the earth beneath her. With her other hand, she unzipped her fleece and the vest she wore underneath, then lifted the remaining layers to expose her breasts to the frigid river air.

Breathless from a combination of the vibrant cold air against her skin, the energy of the surrounding nature that seemed to be infusing her very cells, and the fiery risk of exposing herself to the wide-open winter, Sherry pushed two fingers into her pussy, penetrating herself at a slow pace that nonetheless soon had her breathing heavily, writhing and arching and squeezing her breasts as she pulled her fingers out and pressed her clit, astonished by how close she was to coming with none of the usual frenzy of motion. The slow, pulsing stimulation of the earth and her own hand rose like liquid heat in her until she was gasping, shuddering, coming with a shout that echoed over the deserted landscape. The climax slid through her like a slow, giant wave, covering her in ecstasy until her hands slipped from her body to the frozen surface beneath her.

Gathering herself, she pulled her leggings back into place and sat up, repositioning her camisole and the accompanying layers and pulling on her gloves. Gazing around at the land she was very close to leaving, Sherry felt a gratitude beyond what she ever remembered knowing. The vastness, the mystery, the infinite, breathtaking beauty of this place felt like it could crack her in two.

At that moment, it was hard to imagine ever going back home.

"Mr. Wyatt, one of the gentlemen staying here, came down a little while ago and asked that I give this to you whenever you checked out," Kevin said an hour later as he handed her a well-taped Styrofoam box. "I didn't mention to him that would be today," he added.

"What is it?"

"Given that it was in their freezer storage, I'd guess it's from one of their ice-fishing expeditions. He left a note with it." Kevin nodded at an envelope Sherry hadn't noticed. "If you want to take the note, I can put the package back in the freezer and have it shipped home to you tomorrow."

"Thank you so much." Sherry slid the envelope off the top of the package and pushed it into her purse before paying the balance for her stay and the shipping. As she rolled her suitcase to her rental car, she turned and looked back at the sprawling wooden building one more time. Her breath caught as a strange mixture of yearning and peace suffused her.

It wasn't until she had checked her luggage and settled at her gate that Sherry pulled out the envelope that had seemed to beckon her during her entire drive. She wasn't sure why she hadn't opened it yet. Maybe she felt she needed to attend to reality, the practical matters of checking out and getting to the airport before she allowed herself one more delve into the magic of this place she was about to leave, perhaps forever. Maybe she wanted to save the mystery of whatever the envelope held, as though she could keep Alaska a little longer if she still had this unknown connection to it.

Would he look for her tomorrow? Would he stand on his second-floor balcony hoping to catch a glimpse of her blond ponytail and white ski band heading down to the water? Would he nurse his coffee in the dining room, waiting for her to appear at breakfast?

Taking a deep breath as arousal rose in her core, Sherry pulled the note from the envelope. The date was written at the top, followed by,

Dear Sherry,
Though we know you didn't come to Alaska to socialize,
your presence enhanced our trip. Please enjoy this fresh
salmon (caught yesterday) as a thank-you.
Safe travels home,
Dan, Larry, Stuart, Brett, and Kelsey

There was an arrow at the bottom of the tiny sheet, accompanied by the word *(Over)*. Sherry flipped the paper over.

P.S. You put the whole of Alaska's wild splendor to shame today. (I promise it was an accident—I happened to be taking a solo walk along the river when I saw you. I know I should have retreated when I realized what you were doing, but I couldn't tear myself away from something so breath-taking. ...I hope you will forgive me.)
—Dan

Sherry sat there, unmoving, for a long time, allowing her eyes to touch the words in front of her again and again.

Silent. Still. The moment was both and could not have made clearer that neither was passive. Stillness was not a lack of doing. It wasn't a lack of anything. It was the foundation of all existence, its own silent, vibrant, wholly essential element of being. The opposite of explosion—and just as powerful. And it was winter, with its magical, infinite depth and mystery, that brought such an offering to bear.

Sherry was quite certain she would never dismiss its importance again.

CITY GIRL

"Deep-fried cheesecake?" Isabel gestured at the vendor as we passed to prove she wasn't making the referenced item up. The food at the state fair was, of course, famous, and in the several years since I had been back to attend, the list of offered items had grown exponentially. The category of "deep-fried" in particular seemed to get more outrageous every year.

"I'm saving up for a funnel cake," I said, wrinkling my nose at the idea of cheesecake in deep-fried form. I scanned the food stands that stretched as far as we could see. I remembered funnel cakes fondly as a part of every trip I'd made to the fair as a kid—a classic fair staple, the smell of which still instantly transported me back there any time I encountered it.

Spotting a stand nearby, I started to charge forward but was waylaid by a family with a stroller crossing in front of me. I held up and waited as my body stood coiled, ready to move at the first opportunity. As soon as I began to advance, a couple veered across my path, and I tapped my foot.

"What are you so impatient about?" Isabel said behind me. "We're not in a hurry."

I stopped, feeling the adrenaline chase through me as I stood still. She was right. I stayed in one place until the automatic forward momentum faded.

"I'm not used to the Midwest anymore," I said.

I was startled to realize how true it was. The rushed, impersonal environment I had grown used to for almost the last decade was missing here, and while I experienced it as unsettling in a way, there was a place too where I found it relieving—as well as undeniably familiar. I had grown up among the sedate, grounded undercurrent of the Midwest, unmistakable even amid the energy and extravagance of the state fair.

In the nine years since I'd moved away, I'd been back at least once each year for Christmas, and sometimes more often, but this was the first time in almost as many years that I'd been back while the fair was going on. Though my own days of 4-H projects and prize-winning bell peppers and rooster-crowing contests seemed like a lifetime ago, from the second we'd entered the parking lot, it had felt like just last week that I was here with my two older brothers, perusing the industrial building, prepping for the swine show, going to see everyone from the local country artists on the free stage to George Strait at the grandstand. Every summer of my childhood had included the anticipation of those eleven days in August, and I had continued to frequent the fair, often with Isabel, throughout my high school years and right up through the summer before I left home.

Isabel still looked the quintessential cowgirl in her no-pocket Wrangler jeans and brown, rounded-toe, lace-up boots. When we were younger, we had often looked like twins, side by side in our similar country-girl styles and ubiquitous cowboy boots, all of which we often traded back and forth. My country wardrobe had long since been discarded or donated, down to the last pair of boots I owned up until the day I took off for the East Coast. I'd been leaving that identity behind me, packing up for a shiny new one in the land of skyscrapers and glamour and bustling streets— and, I had found, relentless pacing, ubiquitous traffic, and pervasive pollution. Give and take.

Isabel had offered to lend me a pair of boots for the day. I had taken her up on the offer for old times' sake, pairing the pointed-toe, white-stitched-black-leather style with a pair of cutoffs, a look I'd sported commonly during my teenage years. The outfit soon felt as familiar as the fair itself, and I was grateful for the sturdiness of the steel and leather that hugged my feet as we picked our way over the mud-formed tire tracks and stiff peaks of earth the rain earlier in the week had left on our route to the livestock area.

It was between the sheep and cattle barns that I saw him. He was dressed like a cowboy, which didn't really set him apart around here. The features and physique that made him look like Christian Bale in a black cowboy hat, however, certainly did. My eyes barely had time to run from the black felt to the slate-gray boots he had on before gravitating magnetically to his eyes—which were looking at mine.

My lips parted, and instinctively I took a step toward him. There were twenty-five yards separating us, but I noticed nothing between us as my gaze locked in on him like a laser. It was a focus I didn't even feel like I controlled; it was simply how I looked at people I wanted to fuck.

For a second he held my gaze, and I hadn't determined whether it reflected what was in mine before a wave of people intersected the distance between us, sweeping him from sight as Isabel asked what I was doing and nudged me along. I looked back as we approached the cattle barn, but none of the black cowboy hats in sight sat atop the specimen of masculine sex appeal I had just glimpsed.

As we entered the cattle barn, my focus had already crystallized around finding him. Of course, the probability of such was low; though I now felt content to remain on the premises until my flight back East the day after tomorrow in order to do so, the fair would close before then, and even in the several hours we had between then and now, we were unlikely to encounter him again among the hundreds of acres and tens of thousands of fair attendees surrounding us.

Nonetheless, such logic did nothing to stop the fixation from maintaining a solid grip on me. Large fans blasted furiously from the corners of the animals' stalls as I turned my attention to the cows around us. The air was sticky with the notorious midwestern August humidity, and Isabel fanned her top away from her chest as we walked out the other side of the cattle barn into the searing afternoon sunlight. I blinked and scanned the swirling crowd, an activity my eyes rarely stopped for the next few hours as we perused the karaoke stage, took refuge in the air-conditioned 4-H exhibit building, and stopped for ice cream on our way to the state historic display.

All, alas, to no avail.

"I want to ride the Sky Glider," Isabel said as she polished off her ice cream cone. "That'll take us over to the agriculture building, and then we'll be close to the midway for when it gets dark."

Treetops moved slowly by and then below us as the ski-lift-like ride inched along its suspension. Isabel hung her arm out the side of our bright blue car, tilting her face up to the sun.

"I've always found this ride so relaxing," she said.

"Nothing like being suspended fifty feet in the air in a box by a wire." I was about to comment further when I saw a black cowboy hat beneath us to our left. That wasn't much of a stretch, since there was a ratio of about one black cowboy hat per four people at the fair, but I sensed the distinctiveness of this particular figure and craned my neck to look past Isabel. A jolt sizzled through me as I caught a glimpse of slate-gray boots.

I almost swore out loud, maddened by re-spotting him at a time when there was nothing I could do about it. I glanced at a passing tree, pondering for a split second the effectiveness of dropping into it and climbing to the ground as my cowboy, facing away from us, receded in the opposite direction.

"What are you doing?" Isabel asked, turning toward where I looked as I practically climbed on top of her to keep sight of my visual target. "You see somebody you want to fuck, don't you?" she demanded as she looked back at me. "You have that obsessive look you get when that's become your goal."

I ignored her, trying to discern where Cowboy might be headed as our sky box crept along at the pace of a sloth swimming through honey. As we began to slope downward, a large maple tree emerged between us and the ground, neatly eradicating my view of him.

"Dammit," I swore as I sat back.

"Is it someone you know?" Isabel asked, looking in the direction of the tree.

"Not yet," I said as we approached the disembarkation station. "And at this point I probably won't, since I'm not likely to find him again in this crowd."

"Hard as I know you'll try to," Isabel said cheerfully as we stepped off the ride. I glowered at her as she linked arms with me, turning us toward the agricultural building as she continued her uninvited monologue. "Well, if you're looking to get laid—which I'm sure you are because I've never known you not to be—I'm sure you'll find someone else among the eighty thousand people here who does it for you. It's like the famous fair food," she added as she glanced at the jam-packed food concourse. "Just about anything you've got a taste for, you can find here."

I didn't respond. Admittedly, Isabel was right; there probably was someone I could find for the satisfactory purpose. But having seen the Christian Bale look-alike, it would be like settling for fast food (or deep-fried cheesecake) after knowing filet mignon was in the vicinity.

"Oh, hey look, it's Lisa," Isabel said, raising her arm and calling out. I turned to see Lisa and two of our other high school friends smile as they headed toward us. It had been a couple years since I'd seen any of them, and we exchanged hugs as the five of us congregated under a large sycamore tree.

Dusk was beginning to hover, and the familiar multitude of lights started to blink on all around the nearby midway. Myriad small, large, clear, and colored bulbs acted like a cued light show as they bounced attention from one attraction to another until the entire area was a gleaming display of twinkle and flash.

I checked out of the conversation for a moment to observe the natural light in the form of the sunset lounging casually on the horizon. Its effortless peacefulness was contagious, and I took a deep breath and felt my body relax a notch as I turned back to Isabel and company.

And there he was. Right on the other side of the path, standing with his friends at the edge of the midway as they engaged in animated conversation. He wasn't looking at me this time, but as I stared, he turned his head. He did a double take as he caught my eye.

I held his gaze, throwing an "I'll catch up with you all later" over my shoulder as I started across the asphalt. I heard the smile in Isabel's voice behind me as she filled our friends in on what I was undoubtedly doing. I didn't turn around, but I could sense the quartet grinning in support at my back as Cowboy maintained eye contact with me while I crossed the expanse between us. As I approached, he took a few steps away from his own friends to meet me at the edge of the path.

"Hi." I held out my hand. "I'm June."

"Travis," he said, shaking it. Sparks shot from where our skin touched to every extremity in my body as he seemed in no hurry to let go. He looked me up and down. "Are you from around here?"

"Visiting," I said. "I live in New York."

He nodded, glancing down at my boots. "I thought so." I raised my eyebrows, and he grinned a little. "You're dressed the part, but I get a city-girl vibe from you somehow. I just guessed you weren't local."

I smiled, finding I had to work slightly to keep the wistfulness from showing in it. Years ago I would have been thrilled by such a comment. I wasn't sure how it struck me now that I seemed so obviously out of place here.

"Does that mean you are?" I asked.

He nodded and named a small town in the southern part of the state, a couple hours away from my own hometown and the fairgrounds themselves.

"So, June." His eyes shifted to the midway. "Can I interest you in a Ferris wheel ride?"

I hid a smile. Travis was looking to break the ice. He didn't understand yet that there was no ice with me—it was long since melted, the water cool and inviting and just waiting for an occupant. *Come on in, sweetheart, the water's fine.*

I leaned toward him almost imperceptibly. "Actually, the Tilt-A-Whirl's a little more my speed."

There was the slightest of pauses before he gave an agreeable nod and gestured impassively toward the midway. The ambiguity of this reception fueled the desire in me, and arousal coiled in my stomach as I fell into step beside him, my borrowed black boots striking the pavement rhythmically.

We entered the crowded midway, where excited screams overlapped the whistles and jingles of various games and attractions, as well as hundreds of multilevel voices. Gears and levers cranked around us as we approached the Tilt-A-Whirl, and we waited in the short line for the current ride to come to an end. Travis pulled a folded stack of tickets from his pocket as he approached the conductor, and our matching boot thumps rattled the metal as we ascended the steps and walked around to a car. Travis stepped back to let me in, flashing me a smile as I slid past him and dropped onto the bench. I watched out of the corner of my eye as he settled in beside me.

"I hope this ride's okay with you," it occurred to me to say.

Travis's grin made me catch my breath, and suddenly there was no longer a question that we both knew what we were doing. "It's fine with me. I just wanted to offer something slow to start with, not knowing what you liked."

The ride began to move, crawling slowly for the first few seconds. "Yeah, I'm more of a wild-ride girl myself," I said lightly as I rested my hands on the silver safety bar.

The momentum built, intermittent screams beginning around us as the ride increased to full swing. I smiled as gravity and inertia yanked us forward and backward, ramming us into each other as our car spun wildly at unpredictable intervals. I let out a shriek as we whipped into an uncontrolled spin that pressed me against Travis's hard body.

He grinned at me, and ride-induced adrenaline rushed straight to my pussy.

My hand landed on Travis's thigh a few moments later as the ride jammed us together again, and I turned my head to maneuver my mouth near his ear. "Do you come to the fair a lot?" I almost had to shout over the noise of the wind, the ride, and the screams of our fellow riders.

He nodded. "My parents own a business that sells farm machinery and livestock equipment. They rent a space in the machinery lot for display, and I help them staff it. So I spend a lot of time here."

Our car jolted, and conversation was suspended as we flew into a vortex-like spiral. I squealed, breathless with laughter by the time the car pitched the opposite direction and held us in a vigorous swing from side to side. I looked back at him.

"I see," I said in response to his last comment. I saw the conductor reach for the lever that would bring the ride to its eventual end, and I moved my mouth close to Travis's ear again. "Well," I said as the ride began to slow, "if you feel so inclined to show me, I'd love to take a look at your equipment." I set my hand on his thigh again and bit my lip as I resisted the urge to slide it up and grasp the bulge I was almost sure would be there.

Travis's jaw clenched, and I saw him reach for my wrist. My breath caught when he touched it, slipping my hand up himself to position it on the hard cock beneath his jeans. My pussy spilled over as our car rose and dipped on the platform, the speed decreasing until we came to a stop.

I shook myself as Travis lifted the safety bar, and we both stood up. We didn't exchange a word as I followed him off the ride and back down the steps. As our boots hit the grass, he took my hand and led me to the edge of the midway, out of the plethora of blinking lights into the quieter fairgrounds, past buildings still lit but lacking the bustle they had claimed during daylight hours.

He walked me into the darkened machinery area, where silence surrounded the motionless collection of metal behemoths gleaming in the sparse glow of the few thirty-five-foot lights near the lot. We walked past cutters and plows and grain augers to a cluster of livestock trailers arranged on the grass.

The smaller-sized, fully enclosed livestock trailer stood mostly in shadow, one corner of the silver metal glowing with the reflection of a distant light. Travis unlatched the door and turned to me. Before I could step forward, he pushed into me and wrapped his arms around my waist as his tongue slid against mine with a promise that left me breathless.

He broke away and gestured in invitation, and I stepped up into the trailer, the echo of boots on metal loud in the hot stillness. Travis climbed in behind me and closed the door. He reached for me in the darkness, his mouth on mine as we lowered ourselves to the floor.

Despite the temperature, the metal against my back was cool, spiking the heat between us with a contrast like sweet and savory together. Travis worked the buttons of my sleeveless blouse, and I arched my back as he pulled my bra off and lowered his mouth to a nipple. I sighed as he reached to pull open my cutoffs.

Backing up, Travis pulled my shorts and panties off, and I gasped as he dove without warning between my legs, his mouth warm on my pussy before I could catch my breath. His tongue was insistent, strong, enthusiastic without being the least bit impatient, and I moaned as it was instantly obvious that Travis was a man who loved to eat pussy. A squeal as spontaneous as the one on the Tilt-A-Whirl escaped me as I squirmed, and my nerve endings started to tingle with the orgasm I knew was imminent. Travis rested a hand on my belly, and I took a breath, feeling suspended for a moment before my shriek shattered the air, my body thrashing against the metal beneath me as I bucked and wailed and clutched at his hair, my voice echoing off the walls of our tiny aluminum chamber.

Travis rose to his knees, ripping open his fly as I panted beneath him. I whimpered at the sight of the rock-hard cock that sprang from his jeans, running my hands over the sheen of sweat that covered my body as I arched my back. He pulled a condom from his pocket, and I smiled.

He noticed. "I like to keep one on me, just in case." His smile was a bit sheepish as he shrugged.

"Seems to be paying off tonight." My voice was breathless. Travis was still for a moment, and so he didn't get the wrong idea—that I felt slighted by the thought of his doing this on a regular basis, or that I was offended by the idea of his being with other women—I told him, truthfully: "I do the same thing."

He grinned back then, and the shared understanding of what we both wanted brought us ironically closer right then, the purity of our connection strengthened by the understood congruence of noncommittal intentions. I took the package from him and ripped it open, and his breath hitched as I slid the rubber down his hard cock. The second I was done, he pushed me back, barely giving me time to whisper, "Fuck me," before he plunged into my body and my hips rose to meet him, his hand cushioning the back of my head against the hard, cool floor.

I moaned as Travis pounded me, the echo of metal reverberating around us. Through the slots in the side of the trailer, I could see the Sky Glider inching along in the distance, and I smiled at the forgotten frustration of hours before when I'd caught sight of him from up in the air.

Travis ran his other hand through my hair, and I turned my head to catch his thumb lightly between my teeth, running my tongue up his salty skin as his pace increased and he came inside me, muffling his groan against my shoulder. I lay beneath him, reveling in the deep relaxation of my body as he kissed my neck gently and lifted himself from me.

We stood and dressed, and Travis opened the door. I jumped to the grass and turned back while he closed it.

"Livestock trailer," he said with a grin at me as he secured the door, nodding at the trailer.

But I knew what it was. I smiled in the darkness. I didn't tell him I was from here, that I had grown up on a farm thirty miles from the spot where we stood. That there was nothing in the rows of giant equipment surrounding us that I couldn't identify. When my brothers and I were kids, we were privy to perpetual reminders not to play on or near the machinery—a reprimand I knew was understandable despite having just quite gloriously defied it.

We walked back out to the gravel path and toward the midway, where we stopped just before the whirlwind of lights and sounds.

Travis turned to me. "Have a safe trip home, city girl," he said, tilting his hat up as he bent to kiss me.

I smiled and kissed him back, bypassing for the last time the chance to correct him. He probably didn't encounter too many "city girls" at the fair, and I'd let him keep the fantasy— even as I knew, deep down, that I wasn't one either. We set off in different directions, and I pulled out my phone to text Isabel. When I looked over my shoulder, he did too, and he grinned and waved. I waved back, both of us bidding goodbye to the "city girl" that was as much a figment of my imagination as it was of his.

SUNSHINE

*H*er dark hair hung long and straight past her shoulders, almost covering one eye as she spoke to the bartender. She neither smiled nor looked grim as she faced forward and waited for her drink.

Sean sidled over to her. Up close, her features were striking, set in smooth pale skin surrounding dark brown eyes. She met his in the mirror behind the bar without turning to him, and he smiled.

"Hi," he said easily. "I'm Sean." He held out his hand.

She faced him at last, looking in his eyes for a beat before shaking his hand. "Kelly." She wore little makeup, and the edge of a tattoo peeked out above the top button of her blouse. He smiled wryly as she caught him looking.

"I'm sorry. I was just noticing your tattoo."

She nodded and casually hooked her fingers over the edge of the purple fabric, pulling it to the side so he could see the full tattoo. It was positioned high enough above her left breast that the move was not inappropriate.

The design was a round clock face, intricate in its twelve Roman numerals and solid black hands positioned just after

7:00. Sean studied the precise numerals and tiny black indicators between each one, struck by their meticulous resemblance to those of a genuine clock. Each hand blossomed from its respective black arm into an elaborate tangle of swirls before returning to a pristine point. The ink around the border gave the impression of a shiny casing, and the entire thing was about the size of a silver dollar.

"Interesting," he said with light curiosity.

"Thanks."

"I've never encountered a clock tattoo before. What made you choose it?"

She was watching him steadily. "It's the time my daughter died. 7:02. My way of showing her I'll never forget her."

Startled by the revelation, Sean took a step back, then immediately regretted it. Kelly smiled a tight, tiny smile and turned to accept her drink as the bartender brought it to her. Sean put a hand up when she got out her purse and ordered one for himself, pulling cash from his wallet and handing it to the bartender. Kelly had paused, and for a moment he thought she would argue, but then she lowered her hands and nodded his way.

"Thank you."

Her voice, like her expression, was even. She had not yet seemed unwelcoming, but Sean found himself more unsure than usual whether his presence was desired. His gaze flicked up to the mirror behind the bar again, where he watched her surreptitiously as she looked away from him toward the sun blazing in through the wide glass window. The lobby doors behind them were swishing steadily, hotel patrons leaving for the day or bustling in for check-in. Sean detected a trace of weariness in Kelly's face that was more than momentary, as though it had been etched in over time. He tried to place what was familiar about her.

"When did she die?" The woman couldn't be older than

thirty, though people sometimes thought that about him, and he had turned thirty-two earlier in the year.

"Two years ago."

"I'm sorry." The words sounded pathetically inadequate, but he wasn't about to not say them. They might not be sufficient, but they were true.

Was she married? Sean looked and didn't see a ring on any of her fingers. Her short, unpainted nails looked delicate somehow, contrasting with the rest of her appearance and everything else he'd seen about her thus far. While attractive, there was an aesthetic roughness about her, though perhaps it was just an impression she gave.

As she faced forward again and took a drink, Sean felt at a sudden loss. He didn't know how to comfort her or if that was what she was even looking for. With a wave of defeat, he opened his mouth to excuse himself. At best, it seemed he was in her way; at worst, he was presenting an unwelcome nuisance.

Before he could speak, she said, "Don't go."

"What?"

She glanced at him, then turned back to her drink. "I know you're about to leave. I don't want you to."

He stared at her. She looked back at him. "I'm not very good at talking to people. It's taken me a while to learn that I give the impression that I don't want them around. Sometimes that's true, but not always." Her eyes flicked to the ground, then to the row of liquors lining the mirror behind the bar. "It's not true now."

Sean blinked. He wasn't sure he'd ever met someone so simultaneously enigmatic and direct. Being around her was putting him through paces he was unused to: in the span of twenty minutes, he'd felt attraction, curiosity, sympathy, awkwardness, defeat, and something like poignancy. Was whatever was going on in this encounter worth what might come out of it?

Even as the question arose in him, Sean was aware he couldn't know the answer. He was surprised to realize it didn't feel as important as he would have expected.

"Well, I—"

She interrupted him by standing up and kissing him. It shocked him more than anything she'd done so far, and she was already pulling away by the time his arms reached around her waist. She turned, leaving him more baffled than ever as she sat back on her stool.

Unsure what to say, Sean angled his body back toward the bar and took a drink. He met her eyes again in the mirror, and this time she held his gaze. Her blouse sat such that her tattoo was about half visible now, and her hands were gathered around the glass in front of her.

He shifted a bit. The suddenness and unexpected intensity of her kiss had caused his cock to harden, and the smell of her hair that now lingered in his memory wasn't helping.

Kelly slid off her seat toward him. Sean backed up to give her room, and she looked up at him.

"What do you want?" she asked.

Sean blanched. What was he supposed to say? As he started fumbling for an answer, the question struck him: What *did* he want?

"I mean, there must have been a reason you came over to talk to me," she continued. "What was it?"

Emboldened by her straightforwardness, Sean went with the truth. "I found you attractive."

"And do you still?"

Sean was waiting to see some form of expression on her face. The evenness it had displayed so far, especially in contrast to the volatility he was experiencing, was a bit discomfiting.

At that moment she shifted, and he felt the heat of her body. Whatever response she may have been seeking, the answer was undeniable.

"Yes."

Her mask slipped then, and he sucked in a breath at the sudden and unequivocal softness he saw. The placidity moved back into place quickly enough, but that moment was like the crack in an invisible door letting in a tiny beam of sunshine. And suddenly what Sean wanted more than anything else was to see it come out again.

"Come upstairs with me," he murmured. Not a demand. A request. Perhaps even a plea.

He allowed himself to hope that her falling into step beside him was an acceptance of it. They walked to the elevator, and by the time they stepped into it, Sean wanted to push her to the floor and cover her body with his. He flushed, the primitive musing feeling utterly inappropriate. He glanced over and found Kelly staring at him. Her eyes seemed to have deepened somehow, and for a second Sean thought he saw the same primitive urge reflected in them. He looked away, working to convince himself he was mistaken before he made an ass of himself.

Seconds later they walked side by side to the room he had checked into only a couple hours before. He opened the door and reached for the light, then turned when he felt her hand cover his before he could flip the switch.

"Leave it off," she whispered.

When they emerged from the entry-way, he saw that the natural light spilling through the half-open curtains made the lights superfluous anyway. He turned to Kelly, and before he could say anything, she was kissing him again, pressing against him this time with an urgency that, though understated, was unmistakable. He reached for the buttons of her blouse as she backed onto the bed and pulled him on top of her.

Kelly reached back and unhooked her bra as her blouse fell open. Her tattoo looked sedately out from her chest, and without meaning to, Sean reached and brushed over it with his thumb, registering a strange tightening in his heart as it reappeared from beneath his skin. His hand slid down and caressed the breast below her tattoo with a reverence that surprised him, and as he replaced the fingers that skimmed over her nipple with his lips, his own touch was more delicate than he'd known it could be.

Kelly's chest surged with her inhale, and he heard her breath hitch as his tongue slid over her skin. Then she spoke.

"You don't have to be gentle with me."

He pulled away at the directive, both startled and somehow not surprised by it. He realized he had been being gentle, not because he wanted to but because he felt like he should for some reason. An uncertainty that was becoming familiar filled him, and he paused.

She slid out from underneath him, and Sean rolled onto his back. As she straddled him, Kelly held his gaze, and he found he had trouble meeting her eyes. Though his erection was straining against his jeans, he felt somehow wrong for wanting her, as though she had enough to deal with without some lecherous bullshit from a stranger.

"If you want me," she said, the look in her eyes now demanding that he meet them, "I'm right here." Her voice dropped to a whisper. "Take me."

It was as though the words reached through and pulled whatever was blocking him right out of him. Sean grabbed her hips, and her breath expelled as he ground himself up against her before lifting her so he could pop his jeans open. She backed off to give him room, and he almost came as she licked her lips, staring down at his cock as it sprang from his open zipper. He gritted his teeth against the urge to shove her head down onto it. He was desperate to be inside her—any part of her. Kelly sent him a sidelong glance filled with an unnerving knowingness.

"What did I just say?" she asked.

"What do you mean?" He was having trouble breathing through the pulsing in his cock, which was demanding attention with little room for intellect.

"I said you don't have to be gentle with me." Still kneeling next to his waist, she shifted so she was facing him. "You want to slam my mouth down on your cock." She said it as though this were undisputed, and Sean sucked in a breath. "You are, for some reason, resisting doing that," she continued. "Why?"

Sean thought his whole body might burst from the combination of arousal and frustration. He felt about as much like carrying on a conversation right then as he did hiking up Mount Everest.

"I don't know," he burst out.

Kelly didn't smile. Shrugging, she said, "Have it your way, then. Put your hands behind your head." He did as she said. "Keep them there. But know that what I wanted was for you to grab my hair with both hands and fuck my throat."

Her words made his cock almost hurt, and he couldn't hold back the sharp moan that escaped him. Kelly reached out and ran her fingers lightly up his hard length, and Sean thought he might cry. When she looked at him again, a smile played around her lips.

The next instant her warm mouth was covering him, taking him to the back of her throat, and he clenched his teeth and did everything he could not to come. Kelly arched her back, stretching her lithe body and lifting one leg over him so her pussy came to rest right above his face. As though the energy of not climaxing was shooting a fire right back up his core, Sean yanked his hands out from under his head and seized her hips, lowering her velvety folds to his mouth. He took a breath and somehow amassed the precision to tap his tongue against her clit even as her moans against his cock made him feel he might explode. He shuddered beneath her for another few seconds before bucking up into her with a yell, unable to hold back anymore as he emptied himself into her mouth.

Kelly swung around and rose to her knees, and before he could even ask her to, she straddled his face. Sean's tongue found its way back to her clit like a magnet, his full concentration now on bringing out of her what she had just released in him. Kelly gyrated against him, beginning to whimper, and reached and grasped his hair. In the pressure of her hands, he felt the combination of vulnerability and abandon that made him look up, let his concentration slip just enough so that he could see her face, eyes closed, features wreathed into an expression that was somehow hopelessly far away and immediate all at once. Whatever it was, it wasn't a mask this time.

She squeezed his hair, a silent urging, and he knew she knew he had stopped to look at her. He returned to the single-minded desire to make her come. Make her surrender. Make her fly.

And come she did. Seconds, or perhaps minutes—it all became the same—later, her body began to tremble, and he could feel the moment when she lost control and thrashed against him like a flag whipping in the wind, a beautiful, strangled cry wrenching from her throat. Sean held her hips to keep her steady, keeping his tongue in place until her undulations stopped and she seemed to deflate, her sweat-covered body sliding down his until she landed with her head on his shoulder, more as though by accident than by design. He rested his hands on the warmth of her back and listened to her breathing until it evened.

"You still don't know me, do you."

Sean blinked. He wasn't sure how many minutes had passed; it was possible he'd fallen briefly asleep as they'd lain there. Kelly had lifted her head and shifted slightly so she wasn't on him anymore but rather lay on her stomach beside him. He stared at her.

"Pardon me?"

She smiled softly. "That would be a no." He was relieved to see she didn't seem offended by this even as he racked his brain for a recollection of when he might have met her.

She spoke again after a few moments.

"You were at the retirement party for Benjamin Marcus three summers ago at Cobbs Park." She didn't state it as a question, but when she paused, Sean confirmed.

"Yeah, I worked at his company right out of college. He wasn't the CEO yet then, and I worked with him personally on a fairly regular basis."

"My husband at the time had worked at his company a couple years before, and I met you in passing near the fountain. You talked about the fountains you'd just seen in Paris." Kelly ran a hand through her dark hair and flipped it over her shoulder. "I thought that might have been why you spoke to me today. I thought maybe you recognized me."

Sean almost winced in embarrassment. Not only had he not remembered her, he had just managed to engage in quite intimate contact with her and still not realize they'd met before. Of course, now that she'd reminded him, he couldn't believe he hadn't recognized her. He recalled their conversation clearly, how she'd said she hadn't been to Paris but hoped to go someday. He wondered if she had yet.

"You changed your hair color," he blurted.

"Yes, I was blond then."

A recollection accosted him with a sickening jolt. She'd had a little girl with her that day, a high-energy presence with a popsicle and long blond pigtails that streamed behind her as she galloped around the fountain and surrounding grass.

Kelly was watching him, and though he didn't know how, Sean was sure she knew what he had just remembered. Averting his eyes, he found them automatically drawn to the tattoo above her left breast. The intricacy of the hands really was striking.

"You don't have to feel sorry whenever you look at it." He started at her voice, but there was no harshness in her tone. There wasn't even reprimand. "It's not a symbol of sorrow. It's a symbol of love."

Somehow he hadn't expected to hear something so seemingly sentimental come out of her mouth. He looked up at her, and her eyes instantly told him there was nothing sentimental about it. He had never associated love with such stoic equanimity, and once again his experience of her flew in the face of basic notions he hadn't even realized were unquestioned.

"So. You...aren't married anymore?"

"I'm not."

"Why are you here at this hotel?" Sean suddenly realized how odd it was that two local people would encounter each other at a hotel bar. "Don't you live here anymore?" A tiny stab of consternation zipped through him as he said it.

She shook her head. "I moved about an hour and a half away. My sister just graduated from grad school, and I came back yesterday for the ceremony and her party. I didn't feel like making the drive afterward, so I stayed here for the night."

An hour and a half. That's not so bad. Sean was startled to find the thought in his consciousness. Refocusing, he wondered why she hadn't just stayed at her sister's, but something held him back from asking as he glanced at her.

"What about you? Or do you make a habit of hanging out at local hotel bars to talk to women you find attractive?"

Sean flushed and hoped she didn't notice. The idea wasn't unheard of for him. He was glad that in this case he had a legitimate excuse. "My company's holding a conference here for the next few days. I have to be here early to set up each day, so it's easier to just stay here. I was in the bar to grab something to eat before some last-minute prep work. I had just finished and was on my way out when I saw you."

Kelly nodded in acknowledgment and flipped over. She stretched, her breasts thrusting upward with the arch of her pale back, and Sean shifted as his cock hardened again.

"Well, I suppose I'd better get going," she said when her body relaxed.

"Why?" The question slipped from his mouth before he could stop it.

Kelly's gaze with its now-familiar neutrality landed on him. She paused an extra second before she said, "Why not?"

Sean thought he detected more than a casual flippancy in her question. He looked into her eyes, searching for the light he'd seen in the bar. He was only slightly surprised to recognize that the urge to entice it out of her again went beyond the insistent tingling in his cock.

He remembered her earlier admonition that he didn't have to be gentle with her. Without warning he lunged at her, pinning her beneath him as his lips pushed against hers. The tiny shriek that escaped her, half arousal and half surprise, made his cock surge with the desire to be inside her. She pushed up against him, then pulled her lips from his.

"We need a condom," she whispered.

Sean caught her gaze, and he nodded. "Of course." He gave her a quick kiss before pushing himself up. "Just a second." He fumbled in his small suitcase for the box of condoms he had with him, flushing again as he hoped she didn't ask if he brought condoms with him to all the conferences he attended. He did.

As he ripped one open, she held out her hand. He stepped forward and handed her the small package, watching as she pulled the wrapper off and rolled onto her stomach so she was sideways on the bed. She gestured for him to come closer, and he did, stopping with his knees touching the mattress. With a sly glance up at him, Kelly slipped the condom into her mouth and rose up on her elbows. Positioning herself directly in front of him, she opened her lips and slid them down his cock.

Sean's mouth fell open a little. When she pulled back, she smoothed the condom the rest of the way down with one hand and flipped back over.

"That's something you don't see every day," he breathed.

That elicited a little smile from the stunning woman on the bed, and Sean returned it as he climbed on top of her, sliding his sheathed cock against her clit for a few seconds until her breath hitched. Then he sank into her, exhaling as her heat enveloped him. Kelly's legs slid around his thighs as he started to thrust slowly.

When she pushed against him, he acquiesced and rolled over. Kelly sat atop him, keeping his slow pace at first; as he covered her clit with his thumb, however, she bit her lip and was soon bouncing on his cock like a basketball, her breath quickening as he sensed her nearing climax. Seconds later she squealed and fell forward to grab his chest, riding him in a frenzy as the orgasm swept through her.

As it had been the first time, watching her state of abandon was breathtaking. Sean's release burst forth in response as hers subsided. Kelly's body collapsed onto his chest as he gripped her hips, closing his eyes as his orgasm pulsed inside her.

***

SEAN WATCHED as she got dressed.

"Is there anything you need to get home for right away?" he asked suddenly.

Her face impassive, Kelly answered, "No," after a tiny hesitation.

"Would you stay here with me? Tonight?" He felt a tightness inside at the idea of her leaving. "I mean, I have to get up really early in the morning, but…." His voice trailed off. "I suppose you have to work tomorrow too, though, and I don't want you to have to drive an hour and a half to get there." Something inside him deflated even as he said it.

"I'm off tomorrow. I'm a nurse. I don't go back to work until Tuesday afternoon."

Sean's heart jumped a little. "Really? Well, if you wanted, you could stay here tomorrow night, too. I'll be busy all day, but I'll be done by early evening." He looked down, suddenly embarrassed by his eagerness. She probably had things to do, and here he was asking her to sit around in an empty hotel room all day waiting for him. "I'm sorry. I guess you wouldn't want to spend all day here by yourself."

"I'm pretty sure I could find ways to entertain myself," Kelly said dryly. "And quite frankly, I like to be by myself." Sean looked up. Her intent gaze was on him, and the corners of her mouth turned up in a little smile. "But not always."

She stood up. "Yes, Sean. I will stay with you tonight." The smile still gracing her lips belied the formality of the delivery, and he grinned up at her. Spontaneously she let out a giggle, and Sean caught his breath as the sunshine burst through again for the first time since they'd come upstairs. She composed herself quickly, but the brilliance of what he'd seen twice now wasn't so easy to forget. In fact, he wasn't sure he ever would.

"I checked my bag in at the front desk when I decided to hang out in the bar for a while," she said. "I'll go down and get it."

Sean walked her to the door, resisting the urge to grab her and drag her back to bed as she reached for the handle. There would be time. More time than just the next two nights if he had anything to do with it.

He watched from the doorway as she headed down the hall toward the elevator. Her gait was reserved, but it didn't concern him. She had her reasons for the reserve and the impassiveness and the weariness, he didn't doubt. It was the light they covered up that most interested—captivated, if he was honest with himself—him now. Sean stepped back into the room and let the door drift shut behind him, ready to spend his foreseeable future doing whatever he could to make that light shine.

KISSING CASSIE

Cassie had thick auburn hair and a body built on avid high school sports participation the day I walked into what would be my freshman dorm room for the next nine months. Her smile was not just friendly, but somehow friendly in the most sincere way possible. It enveloped me like a warm bath on a chilly afternoon, and I was taken aback by its effect.

"Hi," we said at the same time, and my laugh was almost a gasp of relief. "I'm Gwen."

"Cassie," she said as we shook hands.

The connection was instant, indelible, and unquestionable—at least for me. I recognized later that a greeting on her part that had been more outgoing, more vivacious, would likely have sailed right over my head into the tangle of a world I didn't seem a part of, another unreachable enthusiasm in a strange lifetime of awkward avoidance and missed opportunities. From the moment I met her, Cassie's capacity for effortless grace was on display, and it was remarkable in its unintimidating nature.

As we started to make our beds and put our clothes away,

I swallowed. The idea of having a roommate had had me in knots all summer, and I still had no idea how to broach the subject I needed to. I sat on my bed and squeezed my hands as Cassie opened a suitcase and started to rifle through the neatly stacked clothes inside.

"That's a pretty dress," I said a few moments later as she pulled out a long purple sheath. It was fitted, a deep-grape color with wide shoulder straps and a V-neck and V-back. Very simple, but very elegant. I blushed as I found myself imagining how she would look in it.

Cassie turned from the closet with a bright smile. "Thank you. It was my senior prom dress. I don't really know why I brought it, but I thought I would just in case something formal comes up sometime, you know?"

I smiled. I didn't know. I'd had very few occasions in my life to dress up.

"Did you go to your senior prom? What was your dress like?" Cassie asked.

"I didn't. My parents were busy that night, and I had to watch my brother."

Cassie tilted her head, her expression inquiring. "How old is your brother?"

"He's eleven years younger than I am. He's…on the autism spectrum." I cleared my throat, ready to stop talking about my family life. "Do you have siblings?" I deflected quickly.

Cassie studied me for a second, then smiled and said, "Yes, I have an older sister." She turned back to her closet. "She's getting married in April," she said, her voice muffled as she slid some garments forward and hooked the purple dress on the bar behind them.

I squirmed uncomfortably, trying to think of a graceful way to transition the conversation.

"I haven't really slept in the same room with many people," I blurted out, failing miserably. I almost choked in my hurry to explain. "I mean—" I got those two words out before I stopped short, at a loss.

Cassie had turned to look at me. Her expression was polite, not nearly as dubious as I would have expected it to be. It allowed me to continue.

"I have nightmares," I said in a calmer voice. "Sometimes they wake me up. I'm worried I'll disturb you when you're sleeping."

Cassie looked interested. "Nightmares about what?"

I blinked. I hadn't expected the question. "I don't—I don't really know," I answered truthfully. "I just know they're… awful." The words sounded ridiculous even to my own ears, and I stared at my lap. This wasn't going to work. I couldn't live, sleep, with someone I didn't know. I couldn't be here.

"What happens when you have them?" Cassie asked, and again her voice wasn't filled with the judgment, accusation, or disgust I had expected. When I looked up, her eyes were clear and calm.

"Uh," I swallowed again. "I just…wake up, usually. I think I scream sometimes." This was an understatement. I knew I screamed, both because I had woken myself up doing it and because my parents had admonished me for it when they'd come racing into my room at night.

"Do you sleepwalk?"

I paused. "I don't think so. I've always been in my bed when I've woken up. I just—fight my pillow or wrestle with the covers sometimes." Once when I was fourteen, I had awakened in the midst of ripping a several-inch tear in my brand-new comforter. It was reversible, thankfully, so I had just turned it over and never told anyone. At night sometimes I would look at the naked stuffing that pushed through the surface, exposed in a way it shouldn't be.

"How often do you have them?"

Cassie's neutral line of questioning was grounding somehow. It was much easier to answer straightforward questions than to try to explain what I didn't know how to describe to someone who wasn't speaking or giving any feedback.

"It varies. Sometimes it seems related to what's going on with me, though I don't know exactly how. When they're bad, they can happen a couple times a week. They don't always, though," I added hastily. "I've sometimes gone a while without one."

Cassie nodded. "Have you ever found anything that helps with them?"

My face burned, and I looked away. My parents had not exactly sympathized with the nightmares, acting as though I could control them and was deliberately trying to inconvenience the household by having them. The idea of offering help or looking for solutions had not been in their wheelhouse.

"Not really," I said, gazing out the window.

My first nightmare in our new dorm room that year happened our first week there. It was simultaneously one of the most mortifying and most magical moments of my life.

I was suffocating. I was screaming, or trying to—no sound was coming out. There was heat, fire maybe, roaring toward me, and it was casually going to swallow me. Kill me. Make me disappear. Forever.

When my eyes opened, an angelic face hovered above me. I coughed, trying to catch my breath, my pupils desperately adjusting to the dim light of what I realized was Cassie's bedside lamp.

Cassie was leaning over me, her wavy hair loose and almost touching my shoulders—or maybe it was touching me, I couldn't tell—her dark eyes deep and focused. Her expression held concern, even sympathy. In seconds I realized what had happened, and I closed my eyes and turned my head on the pillow, mortified.

"Gwen?" The sound was like a pure, tiny, silver bell. It cleared the dread smothering the room like a laser of pure sunlight following a storm.

"Sorry," I whispered into the darkness to my right. My eyes were still closed, my throat so dry I could hardly get the word out.

"Can I help?"

I felt her fingertips on my forearm. The sensation pulled me from the abyss from which I'd just awoken into the immediate moment in a way I'd never experienced. Opening my eyes and looking at her, I was at a loss for words, but for different reasons than usual. Cassie's expression hadn't shifted, and I held my breath for a moment to keep tears from appearing.

"I'm so sorry. I usually only have one per night, so that should be it for tonight." I tried to make my voice light and smiled, still working to keep tears back.

After a moment, Cassie smiled back. "Okay. Good night." She gently lifted her body from my mattress, and I immediately missed its warmth and weight.

By the third nightmare, I started giving in to the tears, unable to table the humiliation and dread I felt—not about the nightmares themselves but about exposing someone else to them this way. Cassie wouldn't be able to make it through the semester having her sleep interrupted all the time. She would request a different roommate, and I would have to start all over. But it wouldn't work. It would never work. I would have to go back home.

It was around the fifth or sixth time that it happened. Cassie and I had been roommates for about two months, and as I jerked with silent tears against closed eyes, I felt Cassie smooth a hand over my hair. She had touched me before by that time, numerous times, but something about the gesture stripped away the tightness covering my body that I hadn't even realized was there. My insides softened, my body opened, and something that seemed like maybe my heart started to feel.

Cassie climbed into bed beside me, turned on her side, and gently guided me by my shoulder to turn in the same direction. She wrapped her arm around my waist and spooned me until I found myself asleep again.

When I woke the next morning, Cassie was already up, back from her shower and winding her hair into a bun in preparation for her 8 a.m. English lit class.

"Hey," she said, eyes sparkling and smile friendly as she held her hair atop her head with both hands. I almost cried. How was she still so sweet, so pleasant, after she had had to help me like I was a child who couldn't take care of herself, couldn't even sleep through the night? How did she not hate me?

I used to think the attraction didn't come until later—months later. But maybe it was there then, in the background where neither of us saw it, watching and waiting with its own understanding of when to step forward. Or maybe it formed organically through the kindness Cassie emanated without even seeming to try. I didn't emit such a thing that easily; I didn't seem to do anything as easily as Cassie did. My clumsy attempts at everything from introducing myself to pouring a bowl of cereal had appeared unavoidable for as long as I could remember.

It was just that with Cassie, they didn't seem a reason for rejection.

WITHIN THREE MONTHS, the nightmares had dropped off dramatically. I hadn't had one for weeks by the time I went home for Christmas. While I was there, I had two, and I found myself yearning to get back to the tiny, two-twin-bed room I shared with Cassie that somehow felt far less stifling than the four-bedroom house in which I'd grown up.

When I did, Cassie was talking about her older sister Lily's wedding, planned for that April. She snorted with laughter as she showed me a picture online of the dress she was going to have to wear. Lily's taste ran to the puffy, the gaudy, the ultra-feminine most of us thought had been left behind with the 1950s. The light pink ruffles around the gown's top looked like roses on steroids; even the model's expression seemed to display a hint of mania, as though she wondered how she had ended up with this fabric monstrosity touching her body.

"Well, I know it's not your style, but it's not really *that* bad," I said, giggling. "Maybe you'll even enjoy wearing something different for a change."

Cassie's laughing eyes landed on me. "What a nice way to look at it," she said, surprising me. Was it a nice way? I didn't usually come up with nice ways or things of any kind. A warmth spread through my body as she looked back at her laptop screen.

"I'm sure you'll look lovely in it," I continued. And I was. It didn't matter whether the dress was hideous or not; I had learned through the pestilence of my nightmares that Cassie had a way of transforming whatever she encountered with her very presence. I was sure a puffy pink dress would be no exception.

She rolled her eyes. "I can hardly imagine how I'll look in it. I'd say the same thing about you, though," she said thoughtfully, giving me a sidelong glance.

"What do you mean?"

"Just that if you had to wear some ridiculous dress like this, I'd think you would look great in it too. By the very fact that it was you wearing it. If anyone could make something like this look beautiful, it would be you."

My breath took a few-second vacation, as it often did when Cassie so easily said the kind of thing that was so uncommon for me to hear. She had used the word "beautiful" in conjunction with me before, and she was the first person to have ever done so.

When I could breathe again, I looked at her. She turned her head and met my eyes, and her expression softened so that her lips landed in a graceful, slightly parted smile, her eyes maintaining the steady, intent gaze she had trained on me the first time I'd met her. In those brown eyes this time, I saw something I wanted in a way I had never wanted anything. I wasn't used to wanting, as doing so hadn't usually worked out for me. I didn't know what to do, what to say, how to move. I was frozen.

I didn't kiss her. She didn't kiss me.

But we kissed. Our bodies just seemed to drift toward each other like dandelion seeds on a breeze until our skin was touching, her warmth joining mine to ignite a glowing ember, one I can't say with certainty has ever been extinguished. Her lips were impossibly soft, the kiss unique in its exquisiteness. Not that I had a whole lot to compare it to—but right then I didn't need to. If I had gotten nothing else out of the years I spent attending college, that moment of kissing Cassie would have been enough.

When April came, I accompanied Cassie home to attend her sister's wedding. Her family was well aware of our friendship by then, and no one appeared to think anything of my spending the weekend with her family and filling in as Cassie's "pseudo-date" at the wedding.

Despite how much the nightmares had abated over the course of the school year, I couldn't deny the nervousness in my belly as we traveled to Cassie's hometown. Her parents were hosting a few other members of the wedding party, so Cassie and I were to stay at her maternal grandparents' farm, five miles from the church and reception hall where the wedding would be. As we pulled into the driveway of the large old farmhouse, I found myself fidgeting.

Without looking at me, Cassie took one hand from the steering wheel and slipped it into mine. "You'll be fine, Gwennie."

I smiled a bit, as I almost always did when she called me that. She squeezed, and warmth infused my body.

As it turned out, she was right: we both slept soundly that night in the immaculate guest room's matching twin beds. The next morning, Cassie pulled her bridesmaid dress from the closet. The protective plastic cover rustled as she laid the dress across the embroidered violets that danced along our identical bedspreads.

"I can't believe how hideous this thing is," she muttered. I giggled, knowing she would look spectacular no matter what she thought of the dress. I was so thrilled to have gotten through the night without disruption I would have worn the dress myself without complaint. Just one more night, and we'd be back in the relative safety of our dorm room.

As predicted, the maid of honor looked marvelous in her ruffled pink assignment. The stylist had beautifully arranged Cassie's auburn hair into a French twist. Graceful tendrils framed her face, and her perfectly outlined eyes looked luminous under thick, dark lashes. Cassie didn't wear makeup often, and she certainly didn't need it, but it sure did its job of enhancing what was already beautiful when she did.

The wedding was the anticipated jumble of talking, eating, laughing, dancing, drinking, chatter, and loveliness. Soon enough we were back in the silence of the guest bedroom in Grandma and Grandpa Hendricks's dark farmhouse, our gracious hosts having retired to bed shortly after our return. I pulled off my high heels, and my feet seemed to sigh in relief. Cassie was already wriggling out of the dreaded pink garment she would never have to wear again. She stood in her underwear as it pooled onto the rustic wood floor.

"Ugh," was her only comment as she looked at it and headed for the bathroom.

I slipped out of my own dress and pulled on an oversize T-shirt. When Cassie returned from the bathroom, she picked up her bridesmaid dress and stuck it back on its hanger. As I gazed at the smooth skin of her back, I remembered our kiss months before. I had never questioned it, regretted it, or felt uncomfortable about it, and I was certain she hadn't either. We didn't discuss it, but it never felt like we needed to. It was just a part of our connection, no different from the trips to the cafeteria, weekends hiking at the park, or silent evenings of studying over shared black licorice.

But it hadn't happened again, either.

"Your maid-of-honor dress in my wedding will look nothing like this, I assure you," Cassie said, startling me out of my reverie. I caught my breath as I registered her words.

"It would be an honor indeed to be such a thing," I said. My voice sounded strange.

"Well, duh," Cassie said, glancing over her shoulder as she hung the dress in the closet. "Did you ever think you wouldn't?"

I demurred internally, glad Cassie couldn't see me blush. That kind of presumption wasn't something that came naturally to me. The idea that I meant so much to her was, for a moment, incompatible with speech.

When I returned from brushing my teeth, Cassie had pulled on her nightshirt and was sitting on her bed to remove the numerous bobby pins from her hair. As I watched her, a brazen desire suddenly surged in me, and it took all my will to temper it as Cassie shook her hair out and pulled back the covers. She reached for the lamp, her nightshirt slipping down her bare shoulder as she looked at me.

"Night, Gwennie." Her gaze seemed to linger on mine for an extra second before she clicked the room into darkness.

I didn't answer, instead studying the moonlight that filtered through the sheer curtains as I wrestled the increasingly fierce urge inside me. Even as something compelled me to maneuver out from under the covers and slide from my bed, the cautious part of myself reminded me that I had no pretense for the action as Cassie always had.

My body, however, didn't seem to think that mattered. And for the first time, it was I who slipped into Cassie's bed that night.

Unlike when she came to mine, Cassie immediately rolled toward me, and our lips found each other's in the darkness before even a whisper was exchanged. Her response started an inferno in me that quickly took over. Cassie gripped the sides of my panties, and I wriggled to help her slide them off before allowing her to carefully pull my T-shirt over my head. When her finger entered me, I tried to keep my intake of breath as quiet as possible—the smallest of gasps seemed to slice through the silent farmhouse like a searchlight. Then she had two fingers in me, and my body rode her hand with an almost embarrassing abandon, having never received such attention, much less experienced such bliss. I couldn't keep still as I pressed myself closer to her, harder onto her fingers, deeper into her space, wanting nothing in between us. Cassie's fingers stayed strong, pushing in and out of me rhythmically and softly at the same time. When she started to circle my clit with her thumb, I pushed my face into the pillow to muffle my moans, barely noticing the irony of potentially waking up the household with a different type of screaming. I was almost dizzy with pleasure, and control of my faculties seemed gone.

Cassie eased her fingers out of me, her other hand maintaining gentle contact on my shoulder. I panted into the pillow. Though I was otherwise physically still, I could feel my body internally reaching out to her like a lost child, yearning to feel her back inside of me.

I opened my eyes and looked into her deep brown ones. That beautiful, gentle, open-mouthed smile was resting on her face. Her voice was a whisper as she said, "Have you ever come before, Gwennie?"

My body jolted at her words, wanting her in every way possible. I was sure she knew the answer. Unable to muster the capacity to speak, I shook my head.

"I don't want to make too much noise," she said in a voice so simultaneously gentle and sexy I felt like I would explode. Cassie placed her fingers on my cheek and ran them softly down my face, letting me smell myself in addition to melting under her exquisite touch. "I think we should wait until we get back to campus to work on that."

I nodded, mesmerized by her voice, her gaze, her scent, her warmth, everything about her that in that instant seemed to hold the whole world in its stead. She kissed me softly, and as if of its own volition, my hand found its way to the velvety skin of her breast. Her inhale was sharp, even surprised, and her body twisted toward my hand in a way I sensed was involuntary. I pushed forward and kissed her neck, easing her onto her back as my lips made my way down her collarbone, inching closer to the nipples I now cradled between my fingers. I had no idea what I was doing, but my body seemed to know what it wanted.

It was Cassie who was panting now, and it fueled an unprecedented arousal in me. My lips replaced one of my hands on her breast, and Cassie's urgent fingertips dragged across my shoulder blades, gripping my skin as I moved my head lower on her body. Her back arched, and she emitted a tiny whimper that was unmistakably a stifled moan as I found my way between her legs.

This was unquestionably new territory for me, but instead of nerve-wracking, it was nothing but thrilling as I brushed a finger gently over the lips of her sex, parting them ever so slightly as I reached to follow my finger with my tongue. Cassie's breathing was like a high-caliber engine with the pedal to the floor, and the very experience of something new being free from fear evoked a euphoria of sorts in me. My movements were effortless but deliberate as I explored the magic of her body.

Allowing my tongue to run lightly up to and over her clitoris, I felt Cassie's hands grip my hair as the feverishness of her breathing increased.

"Yes," she hissed as her body pulsed wildly under my mouth. "Right there. Oh God."

Time seemed to stop as I flicked my tongue incessantly, letting it and Cassie's body communicate in a way I couldn't have understood if I'd tried. Eliciting ecstasy in Cassie was perhaps the most sublime thing I had ever experienced, and fatigue was the furthest thing from my mind as I slid a hand over her thigh and eased one, then two fingers into her, relishing the slick warmth that enveloped them snugly.

Though I had never been in anything close to this situation before, I knew when she was going to come. It wasn't so much a physical cue as a simple awareness that a climax was imminent, and in the instant Cassie's breath suspended for a moment, I anchored the pressure of my fingers in her and let my tongue keep loving her as her body surrendered beneath me, trembling and gyrating and squeezing until I felt the wetness seeping between my own legs. She must have grabbed the pillow out from under her because I heard her muffled voice shrieking into it, the faint echoes unlikely to disturb the house's sleeping residents.

When it was over, we were still for a few moments as I listened to her breathing recover. Then I moved up beside her, pulling the covers over us as she nestled her cheek against my bare shoulder.

At length I whispered, "Thanks for inviting me here this weekend."

"My pleasure…literally," Cassie said, and we stifled our giggles in the darkness. "Truly, though, thank you for coming with me. I wouldn't have wanted anyone else by my side. Especially when I had to wear pastel pink ruffles. I'm so not going to do such a thing to my bridesmaids," she added.

Recalling her earlier intimation, I said truthfully, "If I did have the honor of being one of them, I would happily wear whatever you asked me to."

Cassie was quiet for a moment, her fingers stroking my skin where her hand rested on my belly. When she spoke, her breath was warm against my shoulder.

"In all seriousness, I can't imagine having a wedding without you in it."

I felt exactly the same way about her.

IF THIS WERE A MOVIE, now would be where the scene faded out and returned to the present, zeroing in on my expression as I focused where Cassie stood in a predictably simple and gorgeous white gown, her auburn hair cascading around her face and stained glass windows framing her from behind. From my seat in the back half of the church, my eyes traveled over the four young women standing in a row beside Cassie. The only one I knew was her sister, Lily. They wore long dresses of tasteful simplicity in a shade of midnight blue, the perfect complement to the shimmering sheath the bride wore that was reminiscent of the prom dress I'd watched her hang up in our closet the day I met her.

"How do you know the couple again?" George had asked as we'd ascended the stone steps of the church in this town I hadn't been in since my college years. George, the colleague and friend I'd enlisted to be my date, knew little of my past, and the answer had stuck in my throat for a few seconds.

"The bride and I lived together throughout college," I finally managed. "We met when we were roommates our freshman year."

It was hard to believe that was ten years ago. Though in another way, it seemed like a different lifetime.

I had learned in the six years since we'd graduated that I wasn't very good at staying in touch. When I met Cassie, it had been seamless because we lived together. I didn't have to seek her out, ask for her time, her attention…her love. It was just there, literally a way of life back then. Once it wasn't, I didn't appear to know very well how to maintain contact, draw attention to myself, navigate the withdrawal and anxiety in me that led me to shy away from communicating with people, even when I really cared about them and wanted them around.

I'd never stopped wanting Cassie around.

The truth was, I'd almost been surprised to receive an invitation. But even though things weren't as we'd once thought they would be, it was touching to be remembered after all these years. And I'd known the instant I'd seen the elegant font announcing her name that I wouldn't turn down the chance to see her.

The blare of the organ startled me, and I watched as the newlywed couple turned and started back up the aisle, all smiles as a bubbling air of bliss seemed to follow them like a loyal cloud. My gaze never left my former roommate, best friend, and sometimes lover as they progressed.

Just before they passed my pew, Cassie's eyes landed on mine. For a split second she held my gaze, and I was shocked when my pussy, which hadn't felt her touch in years, gave a quick jolt. I took a deep breath. The love that had always been there was still in her eyes, and its effect was stronger than the physical sensation that continued to fizz through my body. I felt myself relax; it was as though she had just climbed into my bed and put her warm arms around me yesterday.

With a secret smile that took my breath away, she broke eye contact without missing a step, and I glanced around, realizing that though to me it had seemed timeless in that magical Cassie way, our moment of connection must have lasted only fractions of a second on the outside.

Stepping into the aisle amid the mass of guests doing the same, I watched the smooth skin of Cassie's back as she approached the church doors. The vision took me back to another wedding, a time of many "firsts" for me that, no matter what else I experienced in this lifetime, I was aware would never be replicated. Though it was the physical domain of her husband now, I knew that somewhere in my mind, I would always be kissing Cassie.

FULFILLMENT

Kristen rifled through the hangers in her closet, looking for a dress to wear to her workplace's formal fundraising gala the following Saturday. As her eyes fell on a floor-length black velvet gown, the fire alarm in her apartment building started to jangle.

With a huff of impatience, Kristen dropped her hand from the hangers and exited the closet. "Come on, Cheerio," she said, her yellow tabby emitting a small meow of protest as she pulled him unceremoniously from his nap on the back of the couch. Fastening his harness around him, she carried him to the door, doing a cursory check to feel for warmth before opening it. It was the third time in two weeks the alarm had gone off in the building. She felt the temptation to stay put and wait it out, but conditioning led her to exit the structure despite the recent literal false alarms.

Outside, the other building occupants were gathering on the grass on the far side of the parking lot, most looking as annoyed as she felt by the interruption. Cheerio struggled as sirens came faintly in the distance, and Kristen held his leash and set him down on the grass. She watched as two fire trucks pulled into the parking lot and let loose a barrage of heavily clothed firefighters that dispersed toward the building—which looked, to her, quite fire-free.

Several minutes later a firefighter ambled up to a nearby group of her neighbors. Though only the front of his face was visible with his uniform on, that part of him was attractive enough to make her do a double take. He said something to the group before making his way to her. Kristen reached to pick up Cheerio, who was oblivious to all but the unexpected opportunity to chew grass in the evening sunshine, as the firefighter approached.

"You probably know the alarm has gone off here several times recently," he said to her without preamble. "It's the same alarm in the same place in the building that's been pulled each time."

"You can tell which actual alarm is pulled?"

"Yes. We're letting people know because if we can figure out who's doing it—probably a kid who doesn't understand the seriousness—we want to let them know it's illegal to pull the alarm without cause. It costs a lot of money each time fire trucks get called somewhere, and it can keep us from going somewhere we might really be needed."

As he spoke, the cat in her arms stretched forward to closer examine the stranger, and the firefighter reached to scratch Cheerio's head. Kristen looked down as the man's strong fingers ran over her cat's fur, Cheerio purring delightedly beneath the massage. There was something endearing about the casualness of the man's attention to her cat, and she swallowed as she realized suddenly how close his hand was to her breast. The vague heat she'd barely noticed forming under her skin shot up a notch.

"Jonathan," another firefighter called, and the man in front of her turned and strode back to one of the trucks without a backward glance. Kristen watched as he climbed into the monstrous vehicle, which in turn began to slowly creep back toward the parking lot exit.

After a moment, she followed her neighbors back into the building. Taking the elevator to the fourth floor, she entered her apartment and closed the door behind her, allowing the still-purring Cheerio to jump to the floor. Kristen knew better than to want the fire trucks to return to her building for any reason, so she wistfully wrote off the chances of ever seeing the object of her admiration again as she returned to her closet.

She tried to ignore the low heat in her belly as she remembered how close the man's hand had been to her body, even if said closeness had had nothing to actually do with her. Reentering the closet, Kristen returned to the task at hand, not completely successful in dismissing the memory of the firefighter's handsome features as her fingers brushed over soft velvet and smooth satin.

***

KRISTEN'S high heels clicked on the pavement as she approached and pulled open the restaurant door. Her work formal event was over, and she hadn't had time to eat a thing at it. She was hungry, and while she didn't usually get takeout from chain sports bars like the one she was about to enter, it was one of the only places still open and was going to have to do for tonight.

She held up the hem of the black velvet gown as she mounted the three steps to the bar area, aware of the stares of the restaurant's patrons. Her attire was not typical for the establishment, and her cheeks turned pink beneath the tumbling ringlets and dangling rhinestones that brushed her jawline as she watched her step carefully. Once up the short staircase, she dropped her dress and paid for her order, shifting her weight from one stiletto sandal to the other as she yearned for the moment she could rip the shoes off at long last. Accepting her takeout bag, she stepped quickly around the man behind her in line and made a beeline for the parking lot.

Juggling the bag of food, her purse, and the fob on her keychain, Kristen managed to drop her keys just as she reached her car. She sighed as she watched them bounce off the curb and land just far enough under the bumper to make reaching for them awkward in a formal dress and heels. She set her food on the hood of the car and began to gather her gown in preparation for the maneuver.

"That's not a job for you right now." The voice from behind startled her, and she turned as the man it belonged to stepped in front of her and crouched swiftly to grab her keys. After dropping them in her hand, he moved back a few steps.

"Thank you," Kristen said.

He nodded and smiled, then looked back just as he'd started to turn away. "You look familiar. Have we met?"

At another time, Kristen would have written the comment off as a line, but she had just found herself thinking the same thing about him. Before she could answer, his eyes narrowed, and he said, "Do you have a cat? A buff-colored tabby?"

Kristen blinked, her surprise at the question evaporating instantly as she realized why he'd asked it. "You're a firefighter. You came to my apartment building just down the street earlier this week." Kristen now remembered the brown eyes and strong features and was thrilled to see more of the body that went with them. She could hardly believe, on the other hand, that he recognized her, given the cutoffs, t-shirt, and ponytail she'd been sporting when they'd met.

When she expressed something of the sort with a self-deprecating laugh, he said lightly, "Beauty need not be decorated to be recognized. Though you do look spectacular tonight, of course."

Kristen's blush returned in full force at the compliments, which, incidentally, she could have easily returned. He was ridiculously good-looking—even more so than he'd appeared in his uniform, with thick dark hair, deep brown eyes, and a body befitting someone whose job required staying in shape. Casting around for something to say, she realized she hadn't introduced herself.

"I'm Kristen, by the way," she said.

"Nice to meet you, Kristen. I'm Jonathan. So, if you don't mind my asking, what brings you to a place like this looking like that?"

"I had a work gala tonight. I didn't get to eat and was hungry." His smile was disarming, and she couldn't help but return it. "What about you?" she asked after a pause, glancing at the takeout bag in his hand.

He chuckled. "Cooking doesn't always fit my schedule. This was the easiest thing for tonight. But I don't appear out of place by virtue of looking like a million bucks."

I beg to differ. Kristen stopped herself from saying the words out loud. She fretted as it occurred to her that, for the second time, she was about to watch him walk away with little to no chance of ever seeing him again. As though he were somehow following her thoughts, Jonathan spoke again.

"Well, I'll let you get going. It was a pleasure to meet you, Kristen," he said as he unlocked the car next to hers. "Perhaps I'll run into you again sometime."

"You know where I live," she blurted before she could stop herself. Jonathan paused, and Kristen plowed forward. "It's apartment 407. If you're not busy tomorrow night, feel free to stop by."

"As it happens, I'm working tomorrow night," he said.

After a beat, he continued, "But I'm free tonight if it's not too late."

"Not at all," Kristen said, trying not to sound breathless. "Any time is fine."

"I'll take this home and change, then, and be over after a while. I'll try to give you enough time to eat," he added with a wink as he slid into the driver's seat.

Kristen caught sight of the takeout bag on the hood of her car and grabbed it, having nearly forgotten it was there. With a wave, she dropped into her own driver's seat and started the car, noting that excitement had displaced the hunger in her stomach.

As soon as she closed her apartment door, Kristen stepped out of her shoes, resisting the urge to throw them in the trash. Unzipping her dress, she put it back on its hanger and threw on a pair of cutoffs and an oversize button-down shirt before sitting down to eat. Barely recognizing what she was eating, she finished quickly and did a hasty cleanup before heading for the bureau in her bedroom. She didn't know how much time she had before Jonathan showed up, and she'd prefer to be wearing something more interesting when he did.

She yanked open the bottom drawer, where she kept her random array of lingerie, vibrators, and other accoutrements. She didn't have an extensive collection of such items, but she had procured a few things here and there over the years. Rummaging through the overstuffed drawer, she smiled as she encountered a silicone dildo she'd bought years before and not made much use of. Moving it out of the way, she started to look for a black and green lace teddy she remembered buying several years before when she caught sight of an unfamiliar black strap. As she pulled it out, she recognized the strap-on harness she'd almost forgotten she owned. Setting it aside, she continued to search through the drawer. Black fishnet stockings…a little over the top for the present circumstances. Pink silk negligee…too fancy. She pulled out a red lace bra and boy shorts set and was examining them when the knock at her apartment door made her jump. Dropping the red lace items back in the drawer, Kristen shoved it closed and ran to the door. The black satin panties she'd been wearing with her dress were going to have to do, though she felt a little silly that her formal hairstyle, makeup, and jewelry were all still in place with the casual outfit she now had on.

"Hi," she said a little breathlessly as she pulled open the door. Jonathan's eyes flicked subtly up and down her, and her stomach buzzed at the unmistakable admiration she saw in them. "Um, sorry. I had time to change my clothes but not much else, obviously."

"You look amazing," he said easily as he stepped into her apartment. "You have that ability to be a knockout both dressed up and in shorts and a T-shirt. Makeup completely optional."

Kristen blinked and again blushed at the compliment. He had a way of offering them that seemed both casual and sincere; there was none of the self-consciousness that might suggest empty flattery.

Cheerio had woken up from his nap on the ottoman and was looking at their visitor with sleepy eyes. "Hey, buddy," Jonathan said, walking over and reaching to scratch Cheerio's head. The cat wasted no time shoving his cheek against his new friend's fingers, accepting the impromptu face massage with a purr Kristen could hear from across the room.

When Jonathan turned back to her, she was in the midst

of a deep breath meant to contain the wave of arousal beginning to engulf her. Perhaps it showed, because without another word, he strode forward and kissed her, sliding his hand around the back of her neck as his lips parted and made way for his tongue to slide slowly against hers. Kristen's body electrified, her nipples hardening as his other hand slid beneath her loose shirt to graze her breasts, his touch simultaneously light and acute.

Breaking away breathlessly, Kristen turned and led him into her darkened bedroom, switching on the low lamp by the bed. As she turned back to him, her breath caught in her throat. The dildo and harness she had set aside while looking through the bureau drawer were in plain sight on the floor where she had forgotten she left them.

Jonathan's eyes followed hers before she could even begin to think of a way to distract him. Kristen barely breathed as she frantically thought about what to say.

He was similarly silent until he turned to her with a playful smile and said, "I hope I wasn't interrupting something this evening."

Kristen let out a breath, her face flaming. "I—oh, God. Those are just…."

Jonathan shrugged. "You don't need to explain yourself to me. Really."

"But," she sputtered, "they're just there because…I was just looking through some things earlier, and I forgot I'd set those aside and left them there."

Jonathan raised his eyebrows, and Kristen's face somehow flushed even more deeply. She almost wished the fire alarm would go off again and interrupt this scene.

Then he said, "May I ask you something?"

She nodded, noting the change in his tone but unable to discern what, if anything, it was concealing or conveying.

"Have you ever used those on a man?"

He met her eyes, and the look in his was a new combination of confident and vulnerable. Kristen's voice seemed to have disappeared, and she searched for it in vain for a moment.

Perhaps Jonathan mistook her silence for offense of some sort, for he cleared his throat and took a step back. "I'm sorry. That's really none of my business."

"It's okay," Kristen said quickly, her voice resurfacing. She weighed her next words carefully but felt the lead he'd offered made her follow-up not excessively audacious: "Is that something you enjoy?"

She was surprised to observe the tiniest bit of relief in his eyes, as though he'd been waiting for the words to emerge without his having to say them.

"Actually," he said, letting out his breath, "I've never done it before. It's just something I've thought about."

Kristen was stunned but certainly not put off by this unexpected revelation. On the contrary, she found herself enchanted by his combination of genuineness, candor, and desire. It was endearing, and she was impressed by his comfort with knowing what he wanted and his willingness to ask for it. Suddenly decisive, she gestured at the bed and said, "Make yourself comfortable," before grabbing the harness and dildo and disappearing into the bathroom.

Once there, she shed her cutoffs, shirt, and panties and slipped the dildo into the harness. She fastened it into place and started to let her hair down, then stopped as she smiled in the mirror at the formal hairstyle, makeup, and jewelry juxtaposed with the stark black straps over her otherwise naked body. She left it all in place and adjusted the dildo slightly.

Kristen hadn't mentioned to Jonathan that she was new to this too. A former partner had been interested in pegging, but they had never gotten to the point of actually trying it.

She'd never even told him she'd purchased the harness. But she had done a little research at the time so felt decently prepared, if not a bit nervous, for what she was about to do. The black dildo protruding from her pelvis was relatively slender and not very long, so she hoped it wouldn't be too much for Jonathan even though this was his first time.

Reaching into the medicine cabinet, she grabbed a bottle of lube. Then she slipped her arms back into the oversize shirt she had been wearing, pulled a hand towel from the shelf, and opened the bathroom door.

She stepped back into the bedroom clad in the unbuttoned shirt, harness, and silicone dildo. Had she been paying attention to it, Jonathan's response when he saw her would have duly flattered her. But she wasn't paying attention to it because she was too taken by Jonathan's own appearance: he had pulled off his shirt and was lounging on her bed in his jeans, hands behind his head and looking every bit like a model on the cover of a romance novel. Kristen's insides fluttered as she marveled that such a sight was currently situated in her bedroom.

He sat up as she moved closer. "You look incredible," he said softly, reaching for her waist as she bent down to kiss him. Her pussy surged at the sensation of his strong hands moving back to slide down over her ass, left bare by the harness's straps.

She broke the kiss and stood up straight, inviting him to do so as well. He obliged, and she undid his jeans and slid them and his boxers down so that he stood fully naked—and very aroused—in front of her.

Given what she'd read about pegging, she found the boldness to ask, "Have you penetrated your ass before? I'm just asking because this could be a lot for you to take if not. It will help me understand what pace to take."

Jonathan had been looking down at the silicone cock

protruding from her body. At her question, he looked up. "Yes. I've used plugs. I've just never…had anyone else involved."

She nodded. "Okay. Just let me know if anything is uncomfortable or if you need me to change the speed, depth, etcetera."

Jonathan nodded. Despite the technical nature of their conversation, his arousal appeared as acute as ever, and Kristen took a breath as she dropped her eyes to his hard cock. She reached down and stroked it as they faced each other, and Jonathan's breath hitched. He leaned forward and kissed the side of her neck, instantly renewing the wetness she had felt gathering between her legs in the living room. She wanted to feel him inside of her.

But she was willing to wait.

Lowering her hands to his hips, she pushed him gently until he turned around, understanding her unspoken invitation and climbing onto his hands and knees on the bed. Kristen slid her fingertips gently over his ass for a few seconds before flipping open the lube bottle. She poured some over his entrance and added a generous amount to the dildo strapped to her body. When she was done, she moved forward to run the silicone over Jonathan's asshole, spreading the lube there liberally.

"Are you ready?" she whispered.

Jonathan had dropped to his elbows, his naked ass presented for the taking. Kristen felt a surge in her core, and at his low "Yes," she pressed the end of the dildo to his opening and waited until he exhaled to give it a little push.

Jonathan breathed slowly as she took her time entering him, waiting a little bit with each inch to make sure he was adjusting comfortably.

"Does that feel okay?" Her voice was low.

"Yes," he breathed, and a reach around his waist found the

cock her fingers brushed against as hard as ever. Kristen pulled her hips back, sliding the slick black cock out before pushing back in and beginning to undulate with a slow, steady rhythm. She watched and listened closely, her hands resting on Jonathan's hips as she stayed prepared for his direction.

Gradually she got lost in the sensation of what it felt like to physically penetrate someone—the assertion, the self-possession, the responsibility it entailed. She'd had no idea how hot it would be. She barely even needed the clitoral stimulation the base of the silicone cock provided every time she drove into him. The primal sensation that rose in her like steam carried her away as she carefully but solidly fucked him. Kristen could barely keep from upping her pace to a frenzy, grunting as she pistoned in and out of Jonathan's ass with true excitement, nearly forgetting that it was he who was presumed to derive pleasure from this act. Soon she gripped his hips hard, breathless as she realized how much more leverage the move gave her over the stimulation of her clit. With every plunge into Jonathan's ass, she ground her body against the silicone barely separating them, moaning as it brought her closer and closer to orgasm.

Jonathan was breathing heavily too, and when she reached around to check his cock, she hissed when she felt its diamond hardness throb against her fingers. She returned her hand to his hip, pushed all the way into him, and gyrated with abandon against the silicone base that was slick with her own arousal, manipulating the movement until she came with a scream, squeezing and pressing and shaking until she could hardly keep standing.

Her legs were still trembling as she urged Jonathan forward on the bed, climbing onto it behind him and continuing to fuck him on her knees. She pushed the silicone cock all the way into him and reached around to grab his real-life cock. He gasped, and Kristen's fingers grew slippery with his pre-come as she fisted his hardness. She slid her hand slowly over him for a few strokes before jacking his cock as fast as she'd been fucking him, delighting in the sound of his ecstatic grunts for just seconds before he came with a roar, his come shooting onto her hand and her bed as she continued to stroke him with the silicone dildo deep inside his ass.

She gently pulled out of him, and Jonathan collapsed on the bed, panting and sweating and looking about as sexy as Kristen could imagine a human male looking. She got up and removed the harness, setting it and the dildo on the towel before rejoining him on the bed. Immediately he rolled toward her and kissed her deeply, starting a resurgence of arousal deep in her belly.

When the kiss ended, Jonathan lay back. "It's funny," he said after a moment. "I never expected my first time doing that to be with someone I'd just met."

"It was my first time, too," Kristen disclosed.

He glanced at her with surprise. "Really? You'd never pegged anyone before?" When she shook her head, he said, "You seemed pretty...adept at it."

"I'd done some research," she admitted. "I got the harness when someone I was dating a long time ago expressed interest in it. But we never got around to doing it."

"How was it that it came to be sitting out on your floor tonight?"

Kristen flushed. "I was just looking through the drawer where I keep it, and I happened to set it and the dildo aside to get them out of the way and forgot about them when you knocked on the door. In other words, I'm spacey and distractible."

"Well, I guess it worked to my advantage tonight," Jonathan said with a chuckle. "It's not as though I was about to walk in here and say, 'I'd like you to fuck my ass with a strap-on and jack me off until I come.'"

Kristen's stomach jumped at the words. If someone had asked her yesterday, she might have said she didn't think hearing such a directive from an incredibly good-looking man would have turned her on so much it took her breath away. And she would have been wrong.

"I'd better get cleaned up," Jonathan said, hoisting himself gracefully from the bed. "I'm guessing we both had another expectation for tonight—at least I hope so—and since I've been wanting to fuck you since the first time I saw you, I'd prefer to fulfill it."

Kristen's nerves electrified at his words, and the tingle between her legs returned in earnest. As she watched him cross the room, she reveled in the novel combination of afterglow and anticipation that preempted phase two of what had become a most unexpected evening.

A FEW HUNDRED DOLLARS

"For instance, I could probably save you a few hundred dollars tonight."

I heard the boldness of the statement as it came from my mouth, and I almost winced. What had possessed me to let that thought slip out loud?

For the briefest moment the charming, even, ultra-collected man who was hosting this party in his mansion paused. But his smooth face remained impassive, and I likely wouldn't have noticed the momentary composure slip had I not been paying so much attention.

"I beg your pardon?" he said.

It was not something I had expected to say to Eric Gallagher, whom I'd met approximately five minutes before. Given his position as one of the most prominent investment bankers in the city—as well as the host of this semi-open-invitation party—I knew who he was, but it wasn't until I'd turned and found myself standing in front of him near the bar that it had become mutual.

He'd introduced himself, and I told him my name as we shook hands.

"And what do you do, Veronica?" he'd continued. His smooth countenance struck me as predictable given his professional post. It was also unmistakably familiar.

"I'm a romance novelist. My publisher is responsible for my invitation here tonight."

"Well, I'm glad to welcome you to my home. One I might have heard of?"

I'd told him my full name, and he'd raised his eyebrows, conveying, in that unflappable way, that he was impressed.

"Well, it's not my genre, but I have indeed heard the name. Congratulations on your success. Seems you've mastered the intricate art of fulfilling people's fantasies." Eric's blue eyes had sparkled as he winked and lifted his glass.

And that was when it happened.

"Thank you. It is something on which I pride myself." I'd looked him up and down, my gaze coming to rest on his as the words slipped from my mouth before I could reel them back in: *For instance, I could probably save you a few hundred dollars tonight.*

Though the comment had come from a sincere observation on my part, the increasing awareness of its audacity in polite company gathered uncomfortably in my throat. Having worked in the industry, I sometimes forgot that it wasn't as openly acknowledged as seemed appropriate to me.

Since it was too late to undo it now, I swallowed my discomfort and responded.

"You strike me as the kind of man who has particular tastes and is willing and resourceful enough to pay for them."

It wasn't an insult. Domination is undoubtedly a skill—some would say an art—and for someone like Eric Gallagher, who cuts to the chase, doesn't have a lot of time to waste, wants to get exactly what he wants without a lot of fuss, and has a whole lot more money than time to spare, finding a professional would be the way to go.

"I see. And how is it you presume to know about my, ah, 'tastes'?" he said politely, the slightest edge of sarcasm blending with the smoothness of his low voice.

"Because I used to be one of the ones who was paid for such things."

His expression changed then, only slightly, and the level of tension between us, unmistakably sexual in nature, went up. Any restraint in the conversation or façade that had been evident on either of our parts—both of which were likely since we had just met moments before—was leveled as we stood staring at each other, neither of us moving.

Eric took my arm then, gently, and led me from the room, not speaking as we turned down a darkened hallway that was obviously not a part of the mansion open to the party. He led me up a flight of stairs without turning on any lights, and at the top he turned right and walked through the second open doorway.

The room was dark. Leaving it that way, he stopped in the middle of it and turned to me. The outdoor fountain lights beamed through the window just enough to make the shapes around us visible. It was bright enough that I could see his expression, just as I didn't doubt he could see mine.

He crossed his arms. "Do you ever still get paid for it?"

I shook my head. "It is not my profession anymore." The success I appreciated as a romance novelist was how I made my living now and why most of the guests here tonight would assume I possessed the status to be here; it was likely none of them would dream that before I had found success at my craft, I'd made my living as a professional dominatrix.

Eric swallowed then, and in that simple, subtle action I saw the vulnerability just below the surface, yearning and desperate to get out.

There was no longer a question that my assessment had been correct.

There was also no question that my implicit offer had been sincere. I didn't get paid for it anymore, and didn't need to, but money had nothing to do with what I wanted to do with this man here and now. The potential of the situation actually presented a dual ingenuity for me: the allowance to indulge both the sexual and the personal.

Pro-domming was often not about sex. And I had found it neither common nor easy to identify men who sought—or at least who disclosed that they sought—what I had provided professionally in a nonprofessional sexual context. Not that I had tried very hard, but the chance to engage in what I'd done countless times as a pro in a way that got me off sexually was not something I had often encountered.

When the job was about sex, it wasn't about me personally or any personal desire on my part. I was a professional, being compensated as such to provide a service. I did so with invariable sincerity, but I was always aware of the importance of recognizing the distinction between the personal and the professional.

Removing such considerations from the equation, and being faced now with a man I knew could easily have been one of my clients back then, I perceived an opportunity that made the tingle in my pussy graduate to a distinct wetness as I stood facing Eric in the darkness.

I stepped forward. Eric met me with a kiss that seared through my body as any and all questions dissolved, the understanding of what we were doing emerging like the pearl from an oyster, clear and pristine and complete.

When the kiss broke, I backed up. He looked down at me.

I noticed the chair against the wall—the perfect kind, which I doubted was a coincidence—and pointed to it.

"Bring it to the center of the room," I said.

He moved immediately, and my breath deepened in anticipation of what I knew I was going to do, my sex beginning to pulse impatiently. The chair was set on the carpet between us, and even in the shadows, I saw Eric's eyes begging for precisely what I was going to give him. I didn't speak, and he nodded at a closet behind me near the door.

"Sit." I barely recognized my voice. It was not the harsh, commanding tone so well-practiced in my professional days, but nor did it sound the way I was used to hearing myself sound. There was a neutrality in it, but with an intrinsic authority that required no trace of force or effort. As though it wasn't really even coming from me.

I turned and went to the closet. Even in the dark, I found what I was looking for as soon as I opened the doors. Carrying bundles of rope, a ball gag, and a knife in case of emergency, I walked back to the chair where Eric now sat. I'd grabbed the box of condoms, too, and I made sure Eric saw me toss it casually to the floor.

Nothing complicated, no fancy rope work—all I wanted was to hold him in place. I secured his hands together behind the seat of the chair and made quick work of binding his ankles to each of the front legs. The gag, one of my favorite components, was last.

"Any final words?" I said lightly, waiting for him to shake his head before I slipped it into place.

I reached behind my neck and unfastened the crystal choker I wore. "This is going in your right hand," I told him, stepping behind the chair to drop it accordingly against his skin. "Your safe signal is dropping it on the floor. Got it?" I moved back in front of him and met his eyes, waiting until he nodded before I proceeded. It was almost a certainty he wouldn't have to use it, but it was something I insisted on having.

I stepped forward and straddled his hips, still standing. I

could smell his aftershave, and I felt the respondent tingle between my legs. The feeling of his solid body beneath mine made my nipples harden, and I took the liberty of aligning them with Eric's eye level. I watched him look, and I reached and squeezed my tits over the satin of my dress, lowering my body onto his lap and grinding hard against the rigid cock under his slacks. I let out a moan, my pussy already clamoring for attention against the pace of slow teasing I was taking.

I gyrated against him, pushing my throbbing clit against his bulk, growing wetter at the harshness of his breath, at his incapacity to articulate anything vocally, to touch me, to do much of anything but receive and be affected by however I and my body were making him feel. The freedom on my part to do whatever I wanted with no interruption was a power play I unabashedly got off on. And this time, what I got off on was front and center.

"Do you like that?" For some reason one of my favorite things was asking questions the recipient didn't have the option to answer. I moved my mouth to his ear and whispered into it. "I like it. I like it so much I want that hard cock I feel in your pants deep inside my cunt. Would you like that? Would you like to have this tight, wet pussy wrapped around your cock?"

Eric breathed heavily, his body twitching as I moved ever more slowly on top of him. I felt his muscles working under me as he automatically tried to move, to grab me, strip me, fuck me, ram his cock into me and pump furiously, using my wet cunt until he came with the roar of release that was building up in him now.

But that wasn't the scenario we had set up. I lifted myself off of him, the cock beneath his slacks pointing shamelessly toward the ceiling. Leaning in, I ran a finger up the smooth silk of his tie before grasping the knot and loosening it a few inches. I undid the top button of his shirt and stepped back. He would be needing all the air he could get.

I turned and walked a few steps away, stopping with my legs slightly spread. I reached behind me for the zipper of my dress and slid it down. The straps slipped from my shoulders, and the dress fell to my waist. My breasts were bare now in the dark room, though he couldn't yet see them. Still facing away from him, I covered them with my hands, squeezing and gyrating a bit as my dress slid to the floor. I stood in a G-string, an article of clothing I'd grown used to and wore not uncommonly now, doubly appreciating having chosen to put one on tonight.

The arousal from this paradoxical position of freedom and control was making me hot and wet and wanting to come. I slid my hands to my hips and turned, watching Eric's eyes fasten on my naked tits until I hooked a finger under each side of my G-string and slipped it off. Returning to his lap, I lowered myself onto it and ground slowly, finding euphoric the knowledge that he wanted to reach up and grab me but was completely powerless to do so. I could practically feel his hardness pulsing against his clothes as I increased my pace, my breasts bouncing inches from his face.

Eventually I was so hot I backed up almost involuntarily. I was aching to come, but as a pre-show for his benefit I held the urge for another moment and turned around and bent at the waist, resting my fingers against the carpet as I let the light from the window shine on my naked pussy. His breath was harsh, and I didn't doubt his cock was roaring like a trapped, hungry lion with a side of antelope dangling outside its cage as he looked at me. The notion made more of the wetness I could already feel on the insides of my thighs surge from my sex.

I turned back around and lowered myself to the smooth carpet, spreading my legs and leaning back against the wall beside the closet. Looking into his eyes in the shadows of the room, I reached for the soaked folds between my legs.

His eyes were glued to that place as I played slowly, dancing my fingers over my skin and watching him literally squirm as I withheld my own pleasure for the sake of teasing him. When I couldn't resist anymore, I pressed my fingers harder, circling my clit with the singular aim of coming. When I did, I panted heavily, working to keep from making noise as my pussy overflowed, spilling the culmination of my orgasm onto the carpet.

I caught my breath for a moment, then stood and walked back to him. I straddled his thighs but remained standing.

"I'm all messy," I murmured close to his ear. "As you may have noticed. Apologies about the carpet, by the way." The look in Eric's eyes said the carpet was not of immediate concern to him. I continued, "I don't want to touch you now because I'll get your pants all dirty."

I looked in his eyes, which were watering a bit with the agony of delayed gratification. Without warning I reached for his pants and pulled his fly open, yanking his cock out of his boxers. The very feel of it in my hand made me want it inside me so badly my pussy clenched.

I reached for the box, slid a condom on him, and stood, naked, in front of him. I ran my hands over my breasts and bent forward over his body.

"Would you like me to fuck you?" My voice was low, my nipple brushing his jaw as I leaned close to his ear. His vocal response was muffled by the gag so that I could neither decipher it nor appreciate its probable intended volume. The tension that flexed and burst forth in his muscles, however, supported my understanding of the answer he'd given. I ran my fingers lightly up his sheathed cock, which twitched beneath my touch.

I lowered my body so that my heat rested against the tip

of his cock. I could almost feel the desire to ravish me emanating from his body, and the arousal I felt at his helpless position made me whimper. I sank down a fraction of an inch, feeling him try desperately to push himself up into me.

"Do you want to fuck me?" My voice was taunting, coy, as my breasts dangled in front of his face. "Do you want your cock in my wet pussy? Is that what you want?" I said it as though I expected him to reply, nearly coming again without even being touched at the power of the teasing question that could not be answered. The cock against my skin felt ready to explode.

I began to ease onto him, and Eric gave a muffled groan. As I took him all the way inside me, I sighed as though I was slipping into the bliss of a fresh bath. I paused for a moment before I rose back up, moving faster as the sensation filled me with a heady satisfaction and the savage desire for more. Within seconds I had accelerated to a frenzy, bouncing uncontrollably on his cock as a muted cry escaped my lips.

I slowed, regaining my composure as I reined my voice back in. It occurred to me that we were so far from the party that the risk of being heard was minimal, but it seemed polite in my position to exercise discretion.

After I caught my breath, I gathered my self-control and stood up. I could just barely discern the muscles in his upper arms trying reflexively to reach for me before I turned and walked back to the closet.

I was pretty sure what I wanted would be in there, and it was. I palmed the small bottle and walked back to Eric, whose energy I could all but feel grabbing at me as I stood between his legs. I flipped the cap open and upturned the bottle over my open hand.

"Some of this will be nice, don't you think?" I murmured as I reached to spread the lube up and down his sheathed cock. His intake of breath was sharp, and his flesh jumped under my touch as I applied not quite enough pressure to make him come while I smoothed the viscous liquid over him.

When I finished, I flipped the cap shut and tossed the bottle on the floor.

"Are you ready to fuck my ass?" I smiled as I met his eyes. Eric's breathing was strangled as his hips flexed, and I turned around and backed into position against his throbbing cock. I braced my hands against my thighs and moaned quietly as I eased him inside of me. His breathing became frantic as I increased my pace, my own breath catching as I slid my fingers across my slippery clit.

I sensed Eric about to come, and I slowed again, hearing the sound of frustration from his throat as I gyrated slowly, his cock all the way inside my ass. I leaned back against his chest, letting my head fall on his shoulder as I ran my hands over my breasts, barely moving as I let his imminent climax subside.

I reached for my clit and stroked it again, gasping as I almost came, finding myself closer than I had even been aware of. I ground on Eric's lap, his cock buried in my ass, and climaxed again, biting my lip to keep the scream in my throat from escaping as his muffled whimper sounded in my ear.

Resuming my balance with my hands anchored on my thighs, I began riding slowly, using all my self-control to increase my pace only gradually, denying Eric a tiny bit longer the orgasm that was raging to burst forth—and that I knew would be all the more electrifying for it.

Finally, I let go, working to a frenzy as I rode his cock rhythmically, my voice escaping in tiny, restrained shrieks. I felt more than heard the roar emerge from him with the come I knew was shooting inside me and the stifled cry that came from his throat. I rode him until I knew it was done, until I felt his body deflate, spent, beneath me, and carefully lifted off of him and turned around, catching my breath as I reveled in the last few moments of this dynamic between us.

I didn't get dressed before I untied him, crouching naked as I undid the black rope around his ankles and released the binding on his wrists. He stayed seated for a moment, stretching his limbs as I located my clothes and dressed in the darkness.

As I stepped into my shoes, I felt him behind me. The weight of my forgotten choker landed gently on my clavicle, and I caught my breath as his fingers worked the clasp at the nape of my neck. I sensed him lower his hands and swallowed as I turned around.

"Thank you."

He nodded and ran his hands down the lapels of his jacket, the polish and confidence returning, but with a new touch of groundedness, a centeredness I had seen the universal signs of countless times but that always displayed itself uniquely. I had been paid for the service of bringing it forth on many occasions, and it was an endeavor I always appreciated. Still, I knew this time was different—unlike when I had been working, tonight had been about what I wanted, about the purity of desire in me that had always been held appropriately in check when I was being compensated as a professional. As I looked in Eric's eyes, I felt intuitively that my own shift as such had altered his experience in ways I wasn't sure I even understood.

"Do you think your guests have missed you?" I wasn't sure how long we'd been up there.

"Probably." His voice sounded different. Things had been cleared out; energy was moving differently, more freely, in him now, and to a sensitive ear it was discernible even in the vocal cords.

It made me smile.

"I'll let you get back to them." I started for the door.

"I hope you'll come again, Veronica." Eric's voice was soft. I turned back, and he met my gaze from where he stood, unmoving, in the darkness. The light from the fountain caught the gleam of his tie, reverted once again to its state of crisp perfection. I smiled, dropping my eyes to the carpet as I turned back to the door.

I did too.

CHANGING TIDES

He'd seen her almost every day since he'd been there. She sat in the same place on the beach every morning, usually clad in a long sundress or what looked like yoga pants and a tunic, with a pale green, broad-brimmed sun hat that may or may not match what she was wearing. She wore sunglasses, so he couldn't tell where her eyes were trained or even what she really looked like. Ray wasn't sure why he'd noticed her. Maybe it was the consistency: she sat in the same area, in the same position, with the same pale green hat on every day and appeared to do nothing. Or perhaps that was it—she didn't have anything to entertain her. She wasn't reading or looking at her phone or even sunbathing. She just faced the ocean and sat still.

Jameison panted as they trudged through the sand, and Ray glanced down to make sure he wasn't overheating. He dropped a hand to ruffle the dog's thick, dark fur. Jameison looked up at him attentively, characteristic doggie smile in place.

By this late in the spring, the population was sparse on the beach at 9:00 in the morning when he and Jameison were usually wrapping up their morning walk. The hordes of tourists that had populated the area only weeks prior had been long gone by the time he and Jameison had pulled up at his brother and sister-in-law's house several days before. *House* was a loose word, given that the structure was just over five thousand square feet. Ray had to acknowledge, though, that it was nice to be related to someone so rich they could live right along the beach in southern Florida, and to get along with them well enough that they offered to put you up when you took a hiatus from work after a deal you'd worked on for six months blew up at the last minute. He supposed he could view that as a silver lining, had he felt any inclination to find one.

They turned around, and as they neared the grove of bushes that blocked the view of the woman's usual spot, Ray found himself wondering if she would still be there. As they crested the grove, he saw her immediately. She was still sitting, but as Ray watched, she stood gracefully, picked up what he had taken to be a towel but now noticed was more like a yoga mat, and prepared to depart. She paused to look out at the water at the moment they passed by, and Ray lifted his hand in a tiny wave. She smiled in acknowledgment, and he faced forward again, watching out of the corner of his eye as she tucked the mat under her arm and headed away from the water and out of view.

Pulling open the door of Bryce and Zoey's screened porch—a "lanai," he'd been informed it was called down here in beach-land—Ray stepped onto the cool tile and went to get Jameison fresh water. The dog lapped it up eagerly as his sister-in-law descended the stairs and hurried into the kitchen.

"Hey," she said in greeting. "I'm running a little behind for my first appointment of the day. Hi, sweetheart," she cooed, stepping forward to scratch Jameison behind the ears, his tongue dripping liberally. She looked back up at Ray. "I'm going to stop at the grocery store on the way home tonight, so text me if there's anything you'd like me to pick up."

"Thanks, Zoe." As a real estate agent, his sister-in-law set her own work hours and was often home much of the day. Ray was very grateful to her for letting him and Jameison share their house for a while on such short notice. She, after all, wasn't related to him.

After she left, Ray and Jameison went back out to the lanai, the latter wasting no time flopping down on the cool tile floor. Despite what should be the relaxing atmosphere of a giant house on the beach and no agenda, Ray found himself restless during this time off work. If he wasn't doing his job, he didn't know what to do with himself. Over the years some people, especially his ex-wife, had commented that he worked too much, but even in this supposed paradise, his fortieth birthday less than three months away, he had yet to find a compelling way to otherwise spend his time. What did people do besides work?

Ray gritted his teeth as he recalled the failure that had brought him here. In his more serene moments, he could recognize that it had been an anomaly in his seventeen-year career. But he hated to fail. Hated it perhaps more than anything. And this deal falling through had been an unambiguous failure.

Leaving Jameison to his floor nap, Ray slipped out the screen door and made his way down to the water. He turned in the direction he and Jameison usually walked, watching the various seashells emerge and recede among the gentle waves that lapped his feet. The coolness of the ocean was invigorating, and he felt his body relax a bit.

When he looked up, Ray did a double take at a woman standing a few dozen yards ahead at the edge of the surf. Her straight blond hair fell past her shoulders, and she wore a strapless black swimsuit with white bands crisscrossing the front. Ray was glad he had sunglasses on so he could stare appreciatively at the long legs and appealing curves belonging to its owner. She was clearly not one of the twenty-something female tourists that graced the sand in their bikinis during spring break, but her form was fit, and she moved with a self-assuredness he'd rarely seen in a twenty-something. His cock stirred as he watched her. She wasn't going far into the water—barely touching it, really—and Ray subtly advanced his pace, hoping to get the chance to speak with her as he happened by.

As the breeze picked up, her hair blew across her face, and she lifted something he hadn't noticed her holding onto her head.

It was a pale green sun hat.

Ray caught his breath. Was this striking woman the same one who sat in flowing dresses and loose-fitting tunics in the morning? Surreptitiously he watched her as she looked down at the sand, shuffling along where the water barely grazed her feet. A stronger wave came in and doused her ankles, and she stopped abruptly, seeming to wait for the surf to recede before turning away from the water and toward the houses along the beach.

As she did, she turned her head slightly and caught sight of him. She paused for a second in recognition before giving him a nod. Ray capitalized on the opportunity and smiled widely, waving as he quickened his pace to reach her. She stopped and appeared to wait for him, her countenance neither inviting nor discouraging. Neutral.

"Hi," Ray said as he approached, extending his hand as he removed his sunglasses with the other. "I'm Ray."

"Sabrina," she said as she shook his hand. "Where's your dog?"

Ray smiled. "You recognize me."

"You've been walking by in the mornings with a gray and black border collie mix for the last several days."

"I have. Jameison is his name. Are you visiting the area?"

"I live right there," she said, gesturing at the house they were in front of, which Ray instantly realized was aligned with where he'd seen her sitting every morning. He blinked, aware of what such a house went for. Despite the fact that his brother and sister-in-law lived in one, he kept forgetting that people rich enough to actually own and live in these houses existed.

"What about you?" she continued. "You must be just visiting since I only started seeing you recently."

"My brother and sister-in-law live a few houses down," Ray said, gesturing in the direction of their residence. "I'm staying with them for a couple weeks. Do you mind if I ask you something?"

"You just did."

Ray laughed, surprised by the vague nervousness he felt. He didn't usually feel nervous talking to people, but something about the woman's self-assuredness combined with her inscrutable demeanor kept him from feeling completely at ease.

He continued, "I've seen you sitting out here nearly every morning when I walk Jameison. But you don't appear to be doing anything. Are you just sitting out here relaxing?"

Sabrina's half smile almost seemed a silent chuckle. "I'm meditating."

"Meditating?"

"It's how I start every day."

"You come out and meditate on the beach every morning? For how long?"

"Usually around forty minutes."

Ray was fascinated. "Do you do that even during tourist season?"

"Yes."

"How does that work? Don't you need quiet to meditate?"

Sabrina offered the biggest smile he'd seen from her yet, though he had the uncomfortable feeling it was one of amusement and that he had just said something inadvertently foolish. Instead of responding, Sabrina changed the subject.

"How old is Jameison?"

"Ten."

She nodded. "He seems to limp a little...or was that my imagination?"

"He has a bit of arthritis," Ray said, a frown flickering across his face. "Mostly due to age, I suspect."

"Would you like me to make a tincture for him?"

"I beg your pardon?"

"I grow my own herbs, and I have a lot of parsley right now. I can make a tincture with it that may help him feel better."

Ray wasn't sure what to say to this unexpected offer. Sabrina appeared to be trying not to smile again, and Ray felt himself flush. "Parsley? Is that safe for dogs?" he said, trying to sound reasonable, if not knowledgeable.

"Yes, but you can look it up for yourself online. That should reassure you. Parsley is known to reduce inflammation. The tincture is essentially parsley tea—parsley that's been steeped in simmering water for several hours. I can then freeze it in an ice cube tray so it can be given to him as ice cubes."

"That's very nice of you," Ray said, touched by the offering.

"It'll steep overnight, so you'll just need to come by tomorrow to pick it up. I'd love it if you'd bring the patient with you," she added. "Where did you say you're staying?"

Ray pointed out the house, and she said, "Oh, Bryce and Zoey. Please tell them hello."

Ray had forgotten what a small place this was and that most people who lived along the beach might know their close-by neighbors. Philly was definitely not like that. Of course, there was no beach there to live along, either.

"Yeah, she meditates on the beach every morning," Zoey said at dinner that night when Ray mentioned meeting Sabrina. Ray flushed as he recalled how much he'd wondered about this "mystery woman" that his sister-in-law could have cleared up in a matter of seconds.

"Do you know her well?"

Zoey shrugged. "Not really. She keeps to herself quite a bit, though she's friendly enough. Her husband died a few years ago, shortly after they moved in. We only met him a couple times."

Ray was startled. "How did he die?"

"I don't remember," Zoey said, her frown sympathetic as she reached for the green beans. "Do you, honey?"

"I don't," Bryce said, grabbing a roll from the basket. "Some kind of accident, maybe? I seem to recall it was unexpected."

The next afternoon, Sabrina appeared on the lanai when Ray and Jameison were halfway up the sand path to her residence.

"Come on in," she called before disappearing back into the house. Ray held the screen door for Jameison and continued through the lanai's open sliding glass door.

Her home was bright, spacious, and immaculate. Sabrina stood at the kitchen counter that looked out over the large living room, her blond hair pulled back into a ponytail. A few loose wisps found their way down to brush her jawline as she pulled a ceramic bowl from a cupboard and began to fill it with water. She was a beautiful woman. Ray didn't know her age but would guess early fifties. Young to have lost a husband.

She greeted him casually, then dropped to a crouch by Jameison. Her body seemed to loosen as she murmured and cooed and ran her hands gently over the dog's shoulders, chest, cheeks, and ears, all while Jameison panted ecstatically and wagged his tail so much his whole back end wiggled with a youthful excitement he hadn't regularly demonstrated in years.

As Ray observed the shift in Sabrina's countenance, he couldn't help but also notice the cleavage her sundress allowed as she crouched in front of him. Swallowing, he forced himself to look away as he again felt a stirring in his cock. He had never found himself attracted to someone so much older than he was, and it made him feel unexpectedly inadequate—he felt silly even wanting her, as though she were obviously too sophisticated and mature to harbor any such desire toward him. Which was likely the case.

Sabrina stood back up, seeming to regain with the movement an invisible composure that all but confirmed his suspicion. She gestured to the bar stools along the island. "Have a seat."

"Do you have any pets?" he asked as he sat down.

"Not right now," she said, opening the freezer. "You don't have to hold him. He's welcome to walk around."

Ray unhooked Jameison's leash, and the dog trotted back to the living room, where he discovered a plush brown dog bed Ray hadn't noticed and promptly curled up in it.

Sabrina saw his questioning look and said, "I pet-sit professionally. In some cases I walk people's dogs for them during the day, and sometimes I take care of cats, dogs, birds, fish, the occasional turtle, when people go out of town. I have a number of clients who rent out their homes here along the beach during the season, and sometimes they leave their pets behind for a while if they travel during that time. When they do, those pets come live with me for a bit."

She twisted a tray of strangely green ice cubes and dropped one into the bowl of water before setting the dish on the floor.

"How long have you been pet-sitting?" Ray asked.

"About four years. I used to work in accounting, and I stopped shortly after my husband died. I fell into pet-sitting by accident when a few friends started asking me to walk their dogs during the day or watch them when they went out of town because my schedule was flexible. What do you do for a living? You're on vacation, I take it?"

A shadow crossed Ray's face, and he clenched his teeth to keep it from becoming a grimace. "Yes. I live in Philadelphia. I had a…setback at work recently, and it seemed like a good time to take a break. I have three weeks of vacation time accrued, so when Bryce invited me to come out here, I thought I'd take some of it with them."

"You married?"

"Divorced."

Jameison got up from his borrowed dog bed and trotted to Ray's feet, where he sat and looked up, tongue hanging out happily.

"He may need to go out," Ray said. "Want to walk with us?"

Their pace along the beach was leisurely, Jameison content to lope through the sand with no sense of urgency. When he veered toward the water, Ray let him lead the way to the edge of the surf.

"He loves the water," Ray explained over his shoulder to Sabrina. She stood back as Jameison pranced along ankle-deep in the ocean for a few feet. After several seconds the dog jumped further out, leaping and paddling in the shallow water as Ray waded in beside him and gave him the full length of the leash. When he turned to say something, Ray found Sabrina much further back than he expected, safely out of the reach of the water. He gave her an inquiring look.

"I'm afraid of the ocean," she said simply.

He looked at her incredulously. "You live along it."

Her mouth twisted into a tight smile. "I'm aware of that. I like the ocean. I appreciate its energy, its sound, its importance. I prefer to be near it. I just don't go in it."

Ray remembered the hesitation she'd seemed to show when the water had reached over her ankles the day before. What a curious fear for someone who lived beachside. He and Jameison emerged from the surf, and the three of them fell into step again beside each other.

"Do you have plans for dinner?" Sabrina asked, facing straight ahead as they trudged up the sand path to her house.

Ray's breath caught. Could she be coming on to him? Glancing at her profile out of the corner of his eye, he decided not. Her manner was as noncommittal as it had been since he'd met her. She was being polite.

He accepted her invitation to stay for dinner and helped harvest much of what went into it from the garden she led him to, which expanded across almost her entire front yard.

"This is quite the garden," he said as she pulled a final lemon from the tree on their way back inside.

"Yes, I spend a lot of time on it. I think the importance of what we eat is underestimated."

Ray found his mind coopting the reference in a way she didn't intend it, and he mentally shook his head to clear it. The fact that the likelihood of what he wanted actually materializing was approximately nil did nothing to dampen the desire in him. That desire being specifically to take her upstairs and bury his cock deep inside her.

Sabrina was as efficient a cook as she was an obviously masterful one, and dinner was in front of them almost before he would have managed to get anything into a skillet. The first bite of poached salmon seemed to melt in his mouth. When he offered the compliment out loud, she smiled a little.

"Thank you. I enjoy cooking, and frankly, it's nice to share it once in a while."

Ray wondered if she was lonely. She didn't really give that impression, but it seemed to him it must be strange to live in such a huge house all by oneself. But he also felt a distinct ignorance where she was concerned. She seemed to know, to be aware of, so much more than he did that somehow he wasn't sure he would understand what went on inside her even if she told him.

They moved out to the lanai as they finished the bottle of wine Sabrina had opened. For a while they were silent, and Ray listened to the ocean a few dozen yards away. Though it was no longer visible in the darkness, he could identify the sounds of the waves swishing in, breaking with a splash, then sliding back out. He had discovered in the short time he'd been there that each noise was distinctive; in combination, they were mesmerizing in their rhythm and consistency.

When Jameison needed to go out, they walked on the sand for a bit. There was little light pollution, the stars seeming to revel in the benefit of having no competition.

"What scares you about the ocean?" Ray asked. He had a feeling he wouldn't have asked during the day. The darkness seemed to lend itself to a lowering of inhibitions; the fact that they could barely see each other made the boldness of the question fall more easily off his tongue.

He sensed her hesitate. He had the feeling she didn't hesitate often.

"Its power," she finally said, barely loud enough for him to hear.

The words silenced him somehow. Turning, the three of them made their way back to the dark lanai. Sabrina had left the light off after dinner so they could look out at the stars without interruption. When they stepped back in, Jameison pranced through the open sliding door and made himself comfortable on the brown dog bed. Ray watched him settle and turned back to his host.

She had not sat back down but was leaning against the beam along the center of the screen wall, studying him with an expression both impassive and slightly more intense than she had offered up to that point. Like her answer on the beach, the look left him inexplicably speechless, as well as at a loss as to what it meant.

He was wondering whether he should speak when she reached up, her gaze never leaving his, and untied the halter straps behind her neck. Her sundress fell forward, exposing her bare breasts, which Ray couldn't keep his eyes from dropping to. He couldn't seem to make himself move as his gaze locked on the flesh he hadn't, seconds before, experienced a wisp of an expectation of seeing.

When he tore his eyes away and raised them to hers, he couldn't help feeling astonished by the stoicism they still displayed. It wasn't that she hadn't shown utter composure during the entire short time he had known her, but there had to be some place, some point, where the seamless neutrality of her movements was abandoned, didn't there? Even in a moment of supposed passion, everything about her was utterly inscrutable. It unnerved him slightly, the same way it had when he'd first introduced himself to her.

With minimal movement, Sabrina pushed the dress now gathered at her waist down over her hips. Ray's mouth fell open a bit. She was naked underneath.

Despite his stupefaction, Ray was aware that his dick was as hard as he could remember its ever being, and arousal and self-consciousness collided inside him with an intensity that made him fumble like a teenager when Sabrina stepped forward and pulled his shirt off with rapid grace and aplomb. Finally gathering the wherewithal to yank his shorts open, he was almost embarrassed by the obviousness of his arousal in the face of her collectedness.

Would she want to use a condom? He certainly didn't have one. As if he had spoken out loud, Sabrina walked to a small shelf in the corner and opened a drawer. From it she extracted a small box of condoms.

"Do you generally keep condoms out on your lanai?" he couldn't stop himself from asking.

"No. I picked them up today," she said with the same matter-of-factness with which she'd first told him her name.

For some reason his cock surged at that. He'd had no idea she'd been interested. "And what made you put them out here?" he asked, curiosity getting the better of him again.

She shrugged in the darkness. "Just a feeling."

They could have been talking about the weather. Ray's cock was throbbing almost painfully, and her disconnectedness was almost distracting him away from it—but not quite. Despite the vulnerability their disproportionate need presented, he wanted her nonetheless.

The wanting made him move toward her, though his movements and even intentions were not premeditated. He didn't know until he was doing it that he would drop to his knees in front of her, and he sensed rather than heard the intake of breath that indicated the movement had surprised her as much as it had him. Before she could collect herself, he moved forward and kissed the skin just above her labia. Her breathing seemed to suspend, and his own increased in pace. He shifted down and touched his tongue gently to her clit, and she fell back a little to lean against the large glass table.

Ray's tongue slid over her clit slowly, and his self-consciousness began to dissipate as her breath became the cadence he followed as he pleasured the body that breathed it. He learned quickly that the more lightly he touched, the more deeply it seemed to affect her. When her legs started to tremble, he grabbed her hips and lifted her the few inches onto the table. She anchored her feet on the matching chairs on either side of him as he barely broke contact with her flesh.

It was that contact, the mere square inch where they physically touched, that held an intimacy, an authenticity, far beyond any look, word, movement they had exchanged thus far. It was there that Ray sensed the beginnings of the release of control he hadn't even realized until that moment was the basis for her neutrality. Guiding this woman to orgasm had become one of the most compelling desires he had ever felt, but even amid the arousal that relegated thought secondary, Ray was aware that it didn't have to do with him, with his "performing" or "doing" something. The fear of failure wasn't front and center as it had often been in such situations.

It was about her. It was all about her.

He wanted to see her release, see the break from whatever self-control held her in such composure and, ultimately, oppression. His cock throbbed as her hands found their way to his shoulders; he felt himself leaking pre-come as her fingers slowly moved up into his hair. Incrementally they grasped it harder, every increase in pressure relaying a move closer to full surrender, as though she was contributing to it and trying to resist it simultaneously. The world converged to the body beneath his lips, the searing flesh that throbbed under his relentless tongue.

When the wave broke, Sabrina half-moaned, half-hissed as her orgasm gushed forward, liquid heat spilling over his chin as she gasped, shook, came—released. Ray kept his tongue in place through the duration, holding her thighs as he lapped up the alchemy of restraint transformed into ecstasy spilling from her body.

When at last he backed up from between her legs and looked up, her eyes were closed. As odd as it seemed given what had just transpired, Ray was struck by the urge to give her privacy. He averted his gaze as he listened to the tempo of her breathing, recognizing she was doing something more than just descending from orgasm. His cock was still hard, wanting her, but he had no inkling of interrupting whatever was happening inside her. He knew, somehow, this encounter would not end with any lack of satisfaction on his part.

Her eyes still closed, Sabrina reached for the condom nearby on the table, and without moving any other part of her body, handed it to him. Obligingly, Ray stood and stretched it over his rigid cock as her chest shifted with breaths that seemed to pull life itself in and out of her.

When she slid off the table, it was seamless and immediate, but it was different from the way she'd moved before. Grace instead of order. She pushed him into a chair and straddled him, and Ray's cock was fully inside her before he'd even completely registered what had happened. He tried to catch his breath as she bounced on his lap, moving with a fluidity that clearly only existed because of what she had just experienced. Yesterday he would have thought someone riding him this way was "taking charge," but nothing in her movement was about control. It was, instead, as though something was flowing forth, channeling a strength and energy as inimitable as the ocean's waves, which weren't trying to control or overpower anything. They were just doing what they existed to do.

Ray wanted to sit there and let her ride him forever, but the snug heat milking his cock was working toward an explosion he knew he would be powerless to resist. When it came, he grabbed her hips, and Sabrina ground into him as the buildup that had begun the first time he'd noticed her on the beach burst from his cock with an intensity that left him almost dizzy.

When his pulsing deep inside her finally stopped, Sabrina held the base of the condom and rose off of him. She picked up her sundress and glided to the threshold of the sliding glass door. Turning back, she saw him still seated and said, "It seems redundant to invite you inside when you just got about as inside as you could possibly get. Asking if you're coming also seems a little belated, so I'll just be straightforward and request that you accompany me to my bedroom and spend the night with me."

She disappeared into the house. Ray stood and started to follow her, regaining at the last second the coherence to grab the open box of condoms from the table. As he slid the glass door shut behind him, he gave a soft whistle, and Jameison sprang from the dog bed and followed Ray happily up the stairs.

ACKNOWLEDGMENTS

In somewhat chronological order:

Thank you to Ashley Lister, whose Erotica Readers and Writers Association (ERWA) columns I pored over as I began to write erotica, allowing me to find him a helpful resource even before I got to know him personally as an extraordinary author, editor, and friend. Thank you to Alison Tyler, who responded to my first submission of erotica with a request to consider the piece for another anthology she was currently editing; while she did not end up accepting the story for that project, her email represented one of the most exciting events of my writing life to that point, and I am grateful for both it and all her subsequent inspiration, accessibility, and professionalism. Thank you to Violet Blue for giving me my first published work of fiction (erotic or not) and to all the editors who have chosen to include my stories in their anthologies—especially Rachel Kramer Bussel, who has done so more than any other.

Thank you to the publishers who have found my writing fit to include in their catalogues, especially Cleis Press, whose erotica and erotic romance anthologies have featured the lion's share of my published work, and 1001 Nights Press, who allowed my dream of my first (and second) single-author published book to come to fruition.

In working with an editor on this manuscript, I could not have asked for a more attuned, astute, professional, knowledgeable, and generous one than Patricia Esposito. I vastly appreciate her help.

Finally, thank you to Carly, whose casual scoff of, "That's it?" at my first attempt at written erotica gave my psyche the instantaneous permission it needed to not hold back…which it hasn't since.

ABOUT THE AUTHOR

Emerald is an erotic fiction author interested in elevating discussion of and attention to authentic sexual experience. Informed by her appreciation of sexuality's intrinsic beauty, value, and holistic relation to life, she is an advocate for sexual freedom, reproductive justice, and the rights of sex workers.

Her short fiction has been published in more than thirty multi-author erotica and erotic romance anthologies from Cleis Press, HarperCollins Mischief, Excessica, Sweetmeats Press, and Stupid Fish Productions. In 2014 she released her first single-author short story collection, *If... Then: A Collection of Erotic Romance Stories*, published by 1001 Nights Press. Her second collection, *Safe: A Collection of Erotic Stories* (1001 Nights Press), won the bronze IPPY in the Erotica category of the 2016 Independent Publisher Book Awards. She has penned numerous blog entries on topics ranging from sexuality and self-awareness to politics, sex work, and reproductive justice for her website, TheGreenLightDistrict.org, and has moderated the Marketing for Romance Writers (MFRW) Facebook group since 2013.

Emerald lives in Virginia with her furry rescue family of two cats (one blind and one three-legged) and two sibling puppies from the no-kill shelter where she volunteers. The majority of her wardrobe incorporates glitter in some capacity.

Contact: Emerald@TheGreenLightDistrict.org

ALSO BY EMERALD

Safe: A Collection of Erotic Stories

If... Then: A Collection of Erotic Romance Stories